The HANGING GARDEN

Also by Patrick White

FICTION

Happy Valley

The Living and the Dead

The Aunt's Story

The Tree of Man

Voss

Riders in the Chariot

The Burnt Ones (Stories)

The Solid Mandala

The Vivisector

The Cockatoos (Stories)

A Fringe of Leaves

The Twyborn Affair

Memoirs of Many in One (Editor)

Three Uneasy Pieces (Novellas)

The Eye of the Storm

NONFICTION

Flaws in the Glass

Patrick White

The HANGING GARDEN

With an Afterword by David Marr

Picador

New York

This is a work of fiction. All of the characters, organizations, and events portrayed in this novel are either products of the author's imagination or are used fictitiously.

 Printed in the United States of America. For information, address Picador, 175 Fifth Avenue, New York, N.Y. 10010.

www.picadorusa.com
www.twitter.com/picadorusa • www.facebook.com/picadorusa
picadorbookroom.tumblr.com

For book club information, please visit www.facebook.com/picadorbookclub or e-mail marketing@picadorusa.com.

Design by Midland Typesetters

Library of Congress Cataloging-in-Publication Data

White, Patrick, 1912–1990.
The hanging garden / Patrick White ; with an afterword by David Marr. — First U.S. Edition.
pages cm
ISBN 978-1-250-02852-5 (trade pbk.)
ISBN 978-1-250-02867-9 (e-book)
1. Refugee children—Australia—Fiction. 2. World War, 1939–1945—Australia—Fiction. 3. Sydney (N.S.W.)—History—20th century—Fiction. 4. Bildungsromans. I. Title.
PR9619.3.W5H36 2013
823'.912—dc23

2012043260

Picador books may be purchased for educational, business, or promotional use. For information on bulk purchases, please contact Macmillan Corporate and Premium Sales Department at 1-800-221-7945 extension 5442 or write specialmarkets@macmillan.com.

Originally published in Australia by Knopf, a division of Random House Australia Pty. Ltd.

First U.S. Edition: June 2013

10 9 8 7 6 5 4 3 2 1

The Hanging Garden has been transcribed from Patrick White's handwritten manuscript and, in the absence of a living author to consult, not edited.

The HANGING GARDEN

Mamma had been taken into the *saloni*. She was sitting talking to the Englishwoman.

'You'll find her a quiet, reasonable child.'

It made the reasonable child feel grave, important, while remaining unconvinced.

She was standing in a smaller room which opened off the important one where callers are received. It was a house of many rooms, whether their purpose was reasonable or not she hadn't had time to find out, but sensed that she might approve of the house, dark and quiet, standing on the edge of this precipice.

She looked down through the closed window, through the leaves of dark yet glossy trees growing out of a wall of rock above the shining water of a small, private-seeming bay. More than anything the water consoled, its light that of the Gulf. She half-expected that if the curtain were to lift she would catch sight of the volcano on the island opposite. But the leaves were unmoved. She was reminded of the trees in the Royal Garden. As she ran past the benches with their officers and girls she heard her feet crunch on the gravel, running through the cool towards the muddy smell of ducks.

'I'm sure she won't give you any trouble,' (Mamma was saying in the *saloni*.)

'Oh dear no, I can see, Mrs—er—Sklavos' carefully, 'I can see she is quite the grown-up little lady.'

Suddenly Mamma burst into tears, through her crying the sound of furniture a rusty stirring and another sort of motion which must have been this Englishwoman's, she had the figure of a dressmaker's dummy.

'It must be a comfort to know she will be on British soil.'

Mamma could have been mopping her tears. 'But we are not British, Mrs Bulpit. Eirene is a Greek.' How strange it was to hear Mamma's voice, as though feeling its way into a foreign language. 'My husband was a Greek—a Greek patriot. And I was Australian before I married. I do not think of myself as British.'

For a moment Mamma's voice made Eirene feel foreign, when she had never thought of herself as being anything at all.

It became interesting. She supposed she ought to go into the room, and hang around, be with Mamma, even if she didn't show herself. Her future guardian made her feel shy.

Mrs Bulpit was sucking her teeth. '. . . Can't expect me not to feel English . . . English-born . . . husband too. Reg came to Australia on leave . . . a W/O in the Indian Army . . . took a fancy . . . decided to settle . . . sick of blacks . . .'

The child realised the woman was looking sideways at her, but vaguely, as though considering in the depths of her mind, whether this child was black too. So the child, who had never considered her complexion till now, sidled partially from view behind the padding of one of the rusty chairs. From above a scroll where greasy heads had rested her eyes could still take stock.

Mrs Bulpit was a pale woman except where the mouth had been painted over. Her forearms, hands, and face could have been moulded from natural marzipan. The lips shone with crimson grease rising to a little bow, they matched the nails in the marzipan hands, one of them lying in a black lap, the other dangling from a sofa arm the colour of age and dust. More than anything, more than the crimson trimmings of her face and fingers, the colour of her hair made Mrs Bulpit noticeable, the little curls with which her head was arranged were of a rich red such as you see in a windowful of new furniture. The curls had a varnished look and though they might have been freshly done they gave no life to Mrs Bulpit's flesh, they only emphasised its dead pallor.

Mamma blew her nose. 'If you have any queries there is my cousin Mrs Lockhart.'

She had almost eaten off the stuff she had put on her lips for arrival. Nothing to compare with the paint Mrs Bulpit used, Mamma's lips looked blenched and bitten.

'You may wonder,' she said in the foreign-sounding English she had begun using in this house, 'why my cousin does not take Eirene. Too many of her own. —Then too, Alison is one of those who does not care for additional responsibility.'

'Nobody can say,' Mrs Bulpit was saying, 'that I haven't a highly developed sense of responsibility.'

'I also thought Eirene, an only child, might feel oppressed in a large family.'

'That is correct. An only child. One myself. And she'll have her playmate. Another little refugee.

He ought to be in presently. Why he isn't? One I told you of . . . English boy . . .'

Perhaps remembering something, Mrs Bulpit withdrew the hand hanging from the sofa arm and plaited it with the one lying in her lap, as though preparing to protect herself against something Mamma might do or say. At the same time what sounded like a wheeze rustled out of the plastic bust of the dressmaker's dummy.

'Nobody is wholly responsible for what they are.' Mamma's voice sounded tired and dull.

Mrs Bulpit sat contemplating this remark. She was at a temporary loss.

While the child's loss felt permanent she wondered whether to stay in the room or leave it for one of the many others, or the now forbidding precipice outside. Though relieved to have avoided the family of Lockhart cousins, she dreaded her meeting with this boy, probably lurking and listening, the other side of a none too solid wall as she was lurking and listening inside her solitary body. Mamma's eaten lips and adoption of a foreign sounding accent showed her she could expect nothing from that direction. If only Papa. But Papa was dead.

'You'll have to admit when you meet him he's a handsome little lad, Mrs—Sklavos. Blue eyes. And the loveliest hair—pale gold . . .'

Papa's eyes were almost black. They crackled with fire when he talked about what he saw as the future. Now the future was a shapeless dread in what was a stockstill present.

She ended up leaving the *saloni*. The darkening house extending behind it was preferable.

He had spent most of the afternoon pitching stones into the water. The glare no longer made him squint. Salt scales had replaced the scurf of his own skin on legs and arms, now the colour of Arnott's Milk Arrowroot. ('Most Australian kiddies love these biscuits, and I expect you will too Gilbert.' He agreed they were—beaut, carefully.) He licked the scales off his left forearm before pitching his last stone. As afternoon faded, long brassy fingers of light extended from the direction of the city. They reached out at him, but fell short, distorted by ripples in mauve-green water inserting themselves in cracks of the gull-scribbled sea wall. A gull on the long slow curve of its flight let fall a squeeze of white almost like toothpaste on the pale hair. By now so dazed by sun, air, dreaming, he barely bothered.

He supposed he ought to go up, or the old girl would start yelling for him. 'Gilbert? *Gilbert*!' It got on his tits since he had started answering to ‘Gil’. And now this girl. He had heard a car arriving at the house above. Car doors. Too far for voices to carry. But he shivered for the sound of the foreign voice he hadn’t heard.

The bombs he hadn’t heard, but knew about, exploded in his sleep. Nigel is gone, they told him, they wouldn’t say dead. And Aunt Gemma. And the woman at the grocer’s on the corner flipping the evening paper into a cornet, pink gums smiling too shiny false. You could believe in the deaths of older people, but not of Nigel, any more than yourself could die. It was too soon. He could not have told: my friend died, any more than I Gilbert Horsfall am dead.

He chafed an arm in the still fierce light of late afternoon, and scratched at the white writing on the wall.

The people who shared his reluctance to speak about death, often for a different reason told him: now that you are in the States, you are safe, all will be well, you will learn the language and become American. On the other hand other Americans said: ‘Too many privileged British children, arrogant little bastards, the other fool sons of bitches are left to the bombs.’ They didn’t want him, any more than he wanted to be American. He liked doughnuts and popcorn, but hated hominy grits.

What he wanted he didn't know. To be left alone, to be himself.

He and the others, seven of them, were in the charge of Mr and Mrs Ballard. The friendly Americans who thought he was there to become American would not have believed they were only in transit to a place like Australia, any more than Mr Ballard could believe in anything American. He wore a permanent squinted smile of disbelief. He shrugged off the airconditioning and squinted more than ever for the heat, running a handkerchief round inside the rim of his dogcollar.

'Thank God for Australia,' Mr Ballard said to his wife, when all the boys were out of earshot, only one wasn't. 'At least it is ours, Emily—home soil. They speak the same language.'

'More or less,' Mrs Ballard said, who had been there already, as a governess, and moistened her long, glistening teeth.

Throughout their enforced stay in the United States, as their papers were tidied up and then during their journey across that continent, Mrs Ballard seemed to wear the same dress, long and straight—knitted out of string, you would have said with a white collar, sometimes with points, sometimes rounded, held together at the throat by a cairngorm. The dress must have been one of a series, Gil Horsfall supposed, of similar dresses, for Mrs Ballard either did not smell, or was too thin and dried up to generate much more than an occasional whiff.

She wasn't such a bad old stick, in spite of the long slippery teeth. She was inclined to go for walks by herself. He had come across her on a cliff's edge, perhaps looking at the view, he could not be sure, and once stock still in a pine forest, as though listening to the nearest, equally rooted trunk, a chipmunk unafraid of her long brown English shoes. On each occasion when she saw him her slow-breaking smile indicated that she might have been preparing to say something. But she didn't. She folded her colourless lips over the glistening teeth. Mrs Ballard agreed with him, as it were, that they should part company, neither having anything against the other. Gil thought how he would have liked to unpin the cairngorm and keep it for a secret. Any secrets he possessed had been left behind in London in the hurry of evacuation, since when he had acquired no more than a turkey's wishbone during an overnight stay in Kansas City.

Mr Ballard ensured that there was grace before meals and communal prayers night and morning. Like a good clergyman's wife Mrs Ballard went along with it, but you could not tell whether she was praying behind her dry breathing. Gil wondered what the other boys prayed. They were a crummy lot. Some of them mumbled as they squirmed on their knees, and there was one thoughtful nose-picker. Gil did not pray. At night he hugged the darkness to him and hoped for protection from the bombs he had neither seen nor heard, but which sometimes exploded in his sleep. Once he had become a corpse until the warden told fellow rescuers this was the body of Nigel Brown.

As the train was slowly pulling out of Tucson Arizona, Mrs Ballard back turned, standing on the platform watching the houses sidle past, the kids farther down the car filling Dixie cups with ice water they didn't need or fooling with the negro attendant. Mr Ballard sat without his hat telling a Rotary member from Chicago, 'All these boys are from wealthy or in some way important families, and my wife and I are doing our bit seeing them through to relatives or friends in Australia.'

'Is that so?' said the Rotary member, not with undue emphasis, but because he had just regurgitated some of the cornbread he had eaten for breakfast. 'They seem a spunky lot,' he said, to do his duty, after glancing back down the car at the gaggle of grey-flannelled young Britishers.

'The father of Horsfall, this little fellow over here,' the clergyman said, 'has a staff job at New Delhi.

Gilbert is a bit on the quiet side. Which way he goes remains to be seen.'

'Which way—how . . . ?' mused the gentleman from Chicago, flatulence getting the better of him.

'Impossible to say how he'd turn out.'

'So long as he isn't one of these nuts who take the ice-pick to decent folks.'

'I'm not suggesting . . .' Mr Ballard blushed for his indiscretion in giving a stranger, an American at that, such an opportunity.

He was about to join his wife on the platform when the stranger saved him the trouble by announcing,

'I gotta leave you, sir. I got the gas awful bad.'

Gil, too, was glad when the Rotary gent had gone to seek relief from his gas. He wondered about the ice-pick, he had never seen one. He was in no way the nut that most other people seemed to be. But which way to go? Would anyone ever tell him? His father was more 'Colonel Horsfall' than his father, his mother a respectful memory in a Kensington flat and a varnished box at St Mary Abbots.

If he didn't feel miserable it was because so much was happening around him. In San Francisco benefactors waylaid them in the street and in spite of the embarrassed protests from the Ballards, carried off the whole party to a seafood restaurant where

Gil Horsfall ordered soft-shell crabs, and the others settled for fried fish.

Snotty Thirkell, the thoughtful nose-picker of prayer-time, said out loud that soft-shell crabs were the most expensive item on the menu.

But his benefactress expressed approval. 'Quite right too. You've got to pay the price for adventure.'

Of all this the Ballards were less than appreciative, but you could not gainsay a patroness whose lizard handbag was stuffed with dollar bills. If it had been England and peacetime, none of it would have happened, the Ballards would have hurried the boys away from anyone so vulgar.

They were always hurrying, chivvying their charges when in motion. Gil in particular was inclined to dawdle because he liked to look at things and plodding back to their modest hotel on their last night in San Francisco with Gil the endmost vertebra of the crocodile tail, a black man waved his cock at him from the dark entrance to a Gothic Tower. So there was all this, and finally the flying boat carrying them to Australia which touched down flipflapping across the flat waters of the bay, at Sydney.

The end of acquaintanceship with his temporary guardians made no great demands on him, there were too many boys for the Ballards to become personal and emotional about any single one of them. In any case, he was not emotional, unless in those secret compartments where he never allowed anyone to enter. True, he might have been preparing on those two occasions when he had come across Mrs Ballard, once on a cliff's edge, and again in a pine forest where each had decided against what could have become a terrifying intimacy. And now at the end, on the pier at Sydney, in a turmoil of luggage, relatives and friends, Mrs Ballard seemed to be avoiding him, as he avoided her. Her string dress looked more than usually unattractive, ruched, shrunken, hairy from prolonged wear, the white collar, grubby from the flight, and harassed by arrival, held together at the throat, not by the familiar cairngorm brooch, but an outsize safety pin.

It was not difficult to avoid her because the person to whom he was consigned had made herself known to Mr Ballard, who was handing over his boys with relief, as though they were parcels, unregistered ones at that.

Gil left his former guardians and the person who was to be his keeper, to exchange the necessary information most of which would be uninteresting if not unbelievable. Already the faces of the other boys his forced companions of so many weeks were closing against one another as a fresh phase of life swallowed them up. So he went and stood on the edge of the pier, on the edge of the harbour, which by now was a sheet of silver that was stitched with details of gulls' wings. There was a smell of weed and shellfish rising as the sea sucked at slimy woodwork underpinning the world of human traffic.

They were crossing the ghost of a great bridge.

'You should see us in better times,' she told him. 'This is the brown-out—for the war.'

He shivered slightly as they bowled along side by side in the taxi.

'Cold, are you? Well, it's winter here. You'll soon get used to everything seeming topsy turvy.'

In fact he felt hot in his English flannel but there was no need to tell her, and soon they were burrowing into the closed fug of the house she had brought him to. He shivered worse than ever.

'This is your new house,' she told him.

His room was larger than any he had ever slept in, furnished with oddments and two narrow beds, one of them made up, the other with a naked mattress on it, as close to opposing walls as they could get.

The room, he soon realised, was not his. It belonged to an enlarged, near lifesized photograph.

'My husband,' she explained needlessly. She had talked about him all the way across.

Knowing his dead host by heart he no more than glanced at the photograph.

'I have some fish fillets for your tea,' she told him while poking at a pan from which a blue smoke was rising. 'What's your favourite fish, Gilbert?'

'Soft-shelled crabs . . .' It was more a murmured memory than a reply to her question.

'Never heard of 'em,' she said firmly, and poked harder at the pan she was tending. 'I hope you're not difficult about your food—not a finicky boy, Gilbert. Mr Bulpit went for plaice and chips when he was at Home.'

Via the warrant officer, she got back to 'the Colonel' and 'Your dear Mother—to who I was devoted—way back from our Indian days—such a thoughtful lady.'

After the fish fillets they really got down to business, at a cane table with brass ashtrays on the kitchen's fringe. Lahore, Poona, Simla, Bangalore, Bombay—all the old Indian names were trotted out, like the echoes from a snapshot album in Kensington. He closed down while she carried on.

There was the pub he had heard about in the taxi.

'Mind you, I don't take to public houses, and never ever played any part except I was there if a lady was needed to smooth things over. Some of those barmaids. Reg—Mr Bulpit—fancied a public—and made a success of the old *Imperial*, then dropped dead—in that same basket chair where you're sitting—while enjoying 'is evenin' cup of Darjeeling.'

She was steaming from resentment rather than grief, for something that had been done to her.

Gil shifted in the dead man's chair and made it creak. 'Why was the clergyman's wife wearing a safety pin in her collar?' Mrs Bulpit suddenly asked.

'Had to keep it together, I suppose.'

He said he would go to bed. The photo-portrait had been hung in such a way that it leaned outward from the wall and threatened to crush any usurper with its vast slab of compressed meat.

Several of the boys were Lockharts and there were others too small to be at school. Lockharts took him down to the lower end of the yard where tree roots had lifted up the asphalt. They asked him what he had come here for. He couldn't help it, he was sent, he said. They didn't want a lot of Poms. He pointed out that he was only one. He talked like a girl, the oldest Lockhart jeered. He hit out at the Lockhart face, which began to jigger and blink as if standing on a fixed spring. Then the lot of them went into action. They rubbed his face in the asphalt where the tree roots had lifted it up.

The bell rang for school, or what might have been the end of a round and they all marched up towards the classrooms past trees dripping blood from their armpit-hair.

Ma Bulpit said, 'You'll find it hard till you know the ropes. Those Lockharts . . . Australians mean well.'

She brought iodine—white, never used anything but. For one dressed permanently in black, she seemed to find peculiar virtues in white—in addition to iodine, port and rum ('Mind you, I'm not a drinker, it's only sociable to join in.')

As she dabbed, the fire shot through his shin and into his eyes. He wasn't crying, only watering.

She broke the news one Sunday morning in the voice they put on to persuade you to swallow your codliver oil or hold out your arm for a poultice, a quick bright threat on this bright morning.

'You'll soon have company,' she said, 'in the house.'

As if he didn't have enough at school. The house was his.

'A little girl about your own age.'

Ma Bulpit went off into a voice to persuade you the codliver oil was over, the poultice not burning into your flesh. School was better and wasn't all that bad since they went behind the boys' dunny to compare him and Bruce Lockhart, and squeezed each other's muscles.

'Irene's mother is Mrs Lockhart's sister,' Mrs Bulpit was sweetening the pill.

'Why don't she go to Lockharts?'

'We mustn't forget our grammar, Gilbert, Colonel Horsfall wouldn't like that. Boys of the educated class don't say "don't" but "doesn't".'

'Well, why doesn't she?'

'People have their reasons,' Mrs Bulpit said, in her voice a mystery remote from the glistening white dishes she was rinsing. 'Irene,' she added, making it extra English, 'has a Greek father—or had, he died.' She sucked her teeth, perhaps remembering 'Your dear mother,' or because death is something nice people don't talk about. 'Anyway, we must all be kind to little Irene. I'm not all that gone on foreigners, but she's a human being, isn't she?'

As he watched Mrs Bulpit drying one of her lustrous plates, he suspected this Irene might turn out black. He had never met a Greek. Her colour worried him less than her trespass on his territory. As for her being foreign, weren't the Lockharts, Mrs Bulpit, his own father and mother, everyone he could think of except himself and his friend Nigel Brown, who had died of a bomb.

As he dawdled up the path on the evening of this intruder's arrival, it was the threat to his innermost life which made him go slower still, not her foreignness, her Greekness, her blackness, but the fact that she might skip down this same path staking a claim to this or that, the sea wall with the writing on it, the little figs (which weren't figs at all) fallen from the dark old trees (the fig things were his to crush if he wanted and did crush hurtfully) any part of the garden which rejected even the midday light, she would come ferreting out the smells which he knew by heart in the undergrowth, laying claim for sure to the broken statue lying with her legs apart in fern, her tits palpitating with what looked like cut-outs of yellow rubber, her head had gone, he had never found it. Would this ferreting girl? He ran some way off the path kicking out, as he always did, against the Wandering Jew and variegated or plain ivy, till he itched and sneezed, and stubbed his toes, not on the head which was rightfully his, but stones and half-rotted roots, to forestall this marauding girl.

Finding nothing he returned to the path, to dawdle slower, offering himself to mosquitoes which were soon pricking, sucking at his ankles; Gil arrived just below the invaded house on the cliff's edge. He drew himself up into what must be the oldest tree in his threatened garden, so old its limbs were tormented, its muscles knotted, its armpit-hair thickened by moisture and colours of mosses, at the point where the trunk branched he had once seen the moon in the rain and dew collected there. When he had dragged himself up into his refuge, he leaned there panting, waiting for Ma Bulpit's voice to jangle with his heartbeats. 'Gilbert? She is here. Waiting.' Then a pause before greater cunning, 'If you don't come quick we'll have eaten up everything I've got for our tea.' He listened to the contracted silence, but nothing broke it, except the squeaking of an early bat.

• • •

As she escaped from the *saloni*, the woman who was taking possession of her is asking Mamma whether 'little Irene has a good supply of warm Combies.' Mamma's voice was dry, terse. 'Eirene has next to nothing,' she says proudly. At the best of times Mamma could take no interest in a child's underclothes. Least of all when they bundled a few things together in a hurry and were driven to meet the motor boat, driven through streets through road blocks, through walls of darkness to the meeting place. The motor boat made the sound stream. The air streamed. Mamma standing in the bows, is watching the last of tears and starlight, she is crying.

A young officer playing with your neck says you must call him Giles. Another of the men, his dark form puts an arm round Mamma's shoulders. Everybody is behaving with exaggerated kindness. Giles's soft man's voice: '. . . a tough little thing, I'd say . . .' I turn my face. It is dark, but starlight catches tears. All the men respect Mamma, crying for Greece, Papa, herself. Falling asleep I wake in someone's rough hairy overcoat, the wind has died, it is suffocating. You can smell what they say is the desert. We are tramping through sand, under fig trees. The men spread out now that they are free. You can't tell Giles from any of the others. Because I am her child Mamma takes my nearest hand, with the other I tear off a twig, the warm sticky moonlit fig milk trickling through fingers.

Mamma's foreign sounding, proud voice is sucked back into the retreating house.

'Of course, Mrs Bulpit, you shall be provided with money for anything Eirene needs. Who would have thought of woollen combinations escaping from the Germans.'

'. . . hard to imagine . . .' the woman was excusing herself.

Mamma had won her trick.

The house has become stationary now. Will the boy appear round a corner or through a wall to challenge my ownership? Because it is already mine. It smells of mushrooms and dust, it is alive with the thoughts I am putting into it. Doorknobs are plasticine to my hand. I could climb into this cupboard and mingle with a dead man's clothes if they didn't smell so nasty-dead.

The house is large enough to run through. Everything shakes, like the earthquake that year on the island, only the drawers do not slither out, lolling like wooden tongues. But a sudden stillness. I am standing in this great room protruding as far as the edge of a cliff. It has been waiting for me: not so still, it is tremulous. I paddle in pools of pale light in the gritty carpet. Are they traps? Is the room a trap? And outside, the suckers of each tree reaching out from the Royal Gardens which Great Aunt Cleone Tipaldou still refers to as the *National* Park.

'Don't touch, don't push, Eirinitsa.' Aunt Cleone's voice sounds perilously frail in this great room, empty in spite of its heavy groaning furniture. The skittering furniture which fills Cleonaki's small *saloni*, her books, her photographs of brothers and sisters, and those of President Venizelos (signed) and the Archimandrite—all must be treated like invalids. Not this lumpish chest in the house which is to become mine, I can hit it if I like, and do. Hit. Hit. I must hit *someone*—or burst out crying. Will the boy come and find me? I have never known boys.

Men have a different smell, even the younger ones like Giles, paddling his fingers in my neck. Would my neck be sharp enough to cut off the fingers if I closed on them? Dreamy fingers. This man leaning out from the wall 'my husband Mr Bulpit' has thick meaty fingers, smelling of tobacco leaves, and pockets in the face where a razor can hardly enter, or the dimple in a chin, dark at the centre like a navel, and the warrant officer's arms glow like a butcher's shop. The moustache, darker in a blond face, almost drops. He could have varnished his moustache before he left for the photograph. Or is it blood? There is nothing to fear, now he is dead. I am the live one, so hungry I could eat a plate of meat—*chirino*, *stifatho*, *brizoles*—stuff it in—bones and all. The wife and Mamma too busy talking money and woollen underclothes to notice. Only the boy will watch. Is he already watching? On this ugly chest a dry wishbone. Drag on this sticky knob and the drawer grinds, hits me in the breast. There is a snotty string spreading on the handkerchiefs, one of them used. Yes, I am watched. It is his room.

All the house, the garden, must belong to one or other of them. There was nothing they could possibly share, the girl knew as the rotten, ricketty steps allowed her access to her garden. It was hers, like the past, those memories of the Royal or National Garden, whichever way you look at it—nothing could destroy her. She must ferret out this boy if he would not face her, and make it clear.

Then she was looking up into the heart of this black tree, her face held flat like an empty plate and his boy's face slanted above her from looking down empty-eyed into her other emptiness. There was no question of how they might fill the silence. The moment before it might have smashed to smithereens below, or dissolved in a stream of spittle from the tree into her mouth, instead the voice floated from out of the house light and girlish as nobody had heard, 'Come away, Irene—Gilbert! Children? Something lovely for your tea . . .'

They were all three seated round the large black shiny table of a dining room you could tell was seldom used because so much was on display, dishes standing on their edges, silver for a wedding, a clock which had stopped between marble columns below a pediment (Greek in fact) the air unbreathed, cleaner than in any of the other dustier, used rooms, the two children heads bowed, the boy playing with cutlery the girl tracing the pattern (or was it her fate?) in a tea-dipped crochet doiley, 'Madame' Sklavos staring ahead with a smile of disbelief as they waited for their hostess to bring whatever she had for them.

Madame Sklavos sighed and still smiling her disbelieving smile suggested 'I expect you miss Mother and Father, Gilbert.'

The boy grunted and raised a shoulder. Because it was only one of those questions they ask children, he did not bother to tell her Mother was dead.

The boy's hair was as pale gold as she had been told, Madame Sklavos noticed. Blond men left her unmoved.

'Don't you think you ought to leave that doily alone, Eirene? You might unpick it.'

She spoke with distaste either for the ugly lace, her dark child, the blond boy, the situation in the dining room, or the whole of life stretching out of and away from the house on the precipice.

'Doiley . . .' Eirene muttered a new word.

She gave the flat mat a pat or slap. The cutlery on either side of it clattered alarmingly.

Their hostess saved the situation. '. . . Hope you like it!' she half-panted, half-giggled from the kitchen. Forestalling the person her words hung in the dining room surrounded by a black line like what they say in a cartoon.

When Mrs Bulpit appeared she was wearing a pair of asbestos gloves halfway up her marzipan arms, her figure stooped out of proportion to the size and weight of the battered pie-dish she was carrying.

‘It’s salmon pie’ she told them, slapping the pie-dish on the sideboard and then seeming to wonder whether the hot aluminium had marked the varnish.

Madame Sklavos was more than ever disbelieving, her chin tilted in that way of hers. Eirene more interested, for something foreign, but Gil Horsfall, a man amongst so many women, gloomed and refused to show what he thought of salmon pies. Mrs Bulpit’s smile had got smeared in the kitchen. Parted from the not so heavy pie-dish she remained humped between the shoulders. There was a smear of sauce on the black dressmaker’s dummy bust. But she remained the optimist.

Eirene recognised the symptoms from having indulged in hope herself, and for the first time felt sympathetic towards her guardian-to-be; out of sympathy she would have liked to force some of the soft vertebrae in salmon loaf from tinned salmon past the greater predominant lump in her throat.

Mrs Bulpit seated herself and was making passes with her fork above her plate. ‘. . . husband’s favourite dish,’ she told. ‘Mind you, he liked his steak—a steak dinner—and meat for tea, if you gave it to ’im. Men must have their meat, wouldn’t you say Mrs Sklavos?’

Mamma quilted her mouth, her cheekbones had taken on a pinched look. The light had made them look blue. She was chilly.

Mrs Bulpit did not expect an answer, 'That's as it may be,' she decided staring rather hard at her salmon loaf, as though she had seen something in it, before her fork dived and she was wrapping teeth and lips round a generous mouthful, sauce bubbling in beads at the crimson corners.

'There's nothing so nourishing as food,' she said between swallows. 'It doesn't have to be sweet. Food is food. You'll agree to that, Mrs Sklavos.' She plucked a hankie from the bracelet of her wristlet watch and mopped at her pronouncement. 'All those Hindu spices . . . and some foreigners cook in oil, pooh! . . . With us it's always plain fare. You know where you are with the British.'

Thus encouraged the boy began shovelling in his salmon loaf. Why not? It wasn't too bad, and he felt empty. He filled his mouth—fuller than he should have to show them, but no-one seemed to notice. He knew how ugly he must look. He swallowed, and after a bit lost interest, except in finishing his tea.

The Greek-Australian woman or whatever she was had laid her fork alongside her untouched food. 'Don't you fancy it, Madam?' Mrs Bulpit found time to ask. Mrs Sklavos was a real pain, the boy could tell. The girl was messing around with her tea, only because someone would have gone for her if she hadn't. She was holding her head on one side, like some governess, to show she was grateful for small mercies. However dark her face, the parting in her hair was white. He had never seen such a straight white parting. He wondered whether she did it herself, or her mother helped.

Just then she looked up. They were looking at each other. Her face sharpened, she was no Miss Adams trying to look grateful. She had probably done her own parting, and if she offered to do yours she would toss back the hair on either side flip flap, with a sharp-toothed comb before finding where the parting went, then dig in the teeth.

It was his eyes that surprised her. She had never looked into such pale eyes. They gave out nothing, like blind eyes, or old people with cataracts. Till they began shifting like shallow water, a thought or two scuttling through the shallows that he would rather have kept hidden from her, that he might have been afraid for her to know.

And wondering had made her less sharp.

The face was round when he had thought it pointed, the mouth lying soft and loose, like one of the brown skinned sea anemones when there isn't a crab anywhere near.

She was making him lose control of his face, his eyes were watering, when he had never meant to let this girl get a hold of him.

It was ridiculous after all, she saw, in this ugly room, nothing to do with Mamma or Mrs Bulpit, or war, or death.

She might have had doughnuts inside her cheeks.

She would burst, she thought.

They were both bursting from deep inside them.

Mouths stretched, they could see each other's teeth. Hers white and even, there was a gap in his and a dob of salmon loaf, would it fly out?

As they shrieked to tear their lungs.

A bomb might have gone off amongst all this dark furniture. Mrs Sklavos closed her eyes, her nerves couldn't stand it, all they had been through.

'Whatever's so funny?' Mrs Bulpit shouted when she had recovered from her alarm, and her teeth had settled back to normal. 'I'm surprised at you, Gilbert. I always thought you was a gentleman.'

He had left his chair, and was rolling around on the floor, as if he had the stomach-ache.

Or poisoned by salmon loaf it crossed her mind. It made her laugh the harder.

Mamma said, 'Stop, Eirene. You're hysterical. At once. *Please*.'

She obeyed more or less, perhaps because she was a girl. Anyway, she settled into a more controlled, gradually spasmodic mewing, above the skewed doiley in front of her. Mrs Sklavos admires the lace. Mrs B explains the doileys have been dipped in tea. 'Effective, aren't they?'

Gilbert Horsfall continued rolling on the floor, bellowing a little longer, before returning to his chair with the black barley-sugar woodwork. He sneezed once or twice and wiped his nose with the back of his hand.

'The idea!' Mrs Bulpit said. She said children get out of hand when there is a war on, she said a joke was a joke *but*, and a bit more in that vein.

The children sat behind their eyelids. They might have been sulking, wondering how much they had given away to each other, if little ripples had not returned from time to time to their cheeks.

Mrs Bulpit had given up her own room to the mother and daughter. She wanted them to feel at home. She would sleep on the lounge, she said. Detecting a martyr, Mrs Sklavos did not protest. She was too exhausted anyway. After looking at herself in the dressing-table glass and stroking up her hair fiercely with extended fingers she took off her dress, prodded the bed, and got into it in her slip.

'Aren't we undressing properly?'

'I'm too tired.'

The scene in the dining room was still jumping around inside Eirene. She felt she wanted to prowl a bit. The owner had left behind a scattering of hairpins, a dusting of face powder. She would have liked to open drawers and doors but Mamma might have opened her eyes.

Instead she prowled in her socked feet (Mamma had not taken off her stockings). She took off her dress, as Mamma had done. She looked very thin out of it, her upper arms, compared with plumped out woman's flesh and her shoulder blades. In the glass the shoulder blades were looking as sharp as Aunt Cleone's ivory paperknife marking the Lives of the Saints. The shoulder blades were unmarked. Nobody had bitten into them. She saw this woman in the naked dress, her back, her shoulders, covered with little red marks, like a rash, or rubber kisses. The woman either didn't know, or didn't care, as she waited for the long black car to pick her up. Black eyelids of the man. The woman folding her umbrella before getting inside.

'Eirene, aren't you coming to bed?' Mamma frowned without opening her eyes.

It was already warm, but sagging, in the bed which had been the Bulpits'. They were still rolling like porpoises as you fitted yourself into a place beside Mamma. Would she want to touch? You could have plastered yourself against her side, deeper if she would have received you, if the warm wave of flesh you were expecting rolled towards you, its perfect darkness lapping around the little sleeping trout you were waiting to become. She did heave a little, to share with you a fleshy moistness, if not the perfect dark curve you were waiting to fit inside.

It was still only Geraldine Sklavos. Her rings hurt. Her suspender pimples. Why hadn't she undressed? Was she waiting to jump up and leave? Were the Germans, or some other enemy going to arrive?

'Oh dear,' she sighed. 'What a lumpy, uncomfortable bed.'

At least she reached down and started peeling off her stockings. And threw them out. Should you take off your socks?

'Those creatures . . .' She began slightly giggling.

'What?' Should you giggle in return?

'Nothing. The bed. It needs—*Teasing*.'

Mamma was heaving like any Bulpit porpoise.

It was too giggly to resist. You were bumping, cannoning off each other, like a couple of older girls with the giggles.

Mamma's sinuses were giving trouble. 'Oh dear, aren't we awful!' She sniffed, bumped and giggled.

If you had a hankie, you could have offered a hankie. If you put your arms, would this other, older girl bump you off? It was worth the try.

But they were off again. 'Those asbestos gloves . . .' the two friends were bumping more than ever.

When a stiffening set in. It was Mamma saying, 'People can't help what they look like, you must remember that, Eirene, and never laugh at physical peculiarities.'

'But the gloves . . .' you might have pointed out, if you had been simple, and Mamma knew you weren't that, unless when it suited her to see you as a child.

'We must sleep,' her sinuses ordered angrily.

And turned her back, and was soon sighing and resisting, trying to free herself, it seemed, of enormous, sticky spider webs.

'Oh no . . .' she moaned, opening and closing, opening and closing, like a knife, you were glad you were on the wrong side.

Welll ssleep. She has a very bad congestion, Great Aunt Cleone said. But you can't cup a little child's body, there is no flesh to fill the vacuum. It is Ayia

Anastasia who has spells to dissolve sickness. We must pray to the Saint, her black robe, her dark face, but remember, Eirinitsa, religion is not superstition. When you are older, the spirit will guide you—the *pneuma*. You will realise the difference. Though Ayios Fanourios is useful—to find things we have lost—except we must bake him a *pita*. It was fascinating. Great Aunt Cleone could not have boiled a potato let alone baked a *pita*. So religion is easier than superstition for people like Cleonaki. She has the eyes of this great Italian actress and Saints. Your *spiritual* aunt, people say. Papa says, '*ah mba*' he accepts the Panayia only when she becomes Greece and they torture her.

My pneumatic *pneuma* is a comfort floating through the seas and forests of dreams. Not Aunt Cleone, not Mamma, not even Papa will recognise this part of me if I float against them. What about him?

Gilbert Horsfall, asleep in that narrow bed, may understand, but spits out lumps of salmon loaf through the gaps in his large, boy's teeth. Saw I knew too much, the dried-up wishbone, the maze of string in the handkerchief drawer. Stir up the handkerchiefs and the mouse squeaks for its little black secrets.

Or float together eye to eye seeing and knowing inside the bluish skin stretched across the moon.

• • •

The blue-grey light inside this room.

'Ah no—it's too early . . .' The grey sheet rustling as you drag it closer.

'But darling, I can't sleep—on such an important day . . .'

Mamma almost never calls you 'darling'. She has put on her dress. She sits down fitting her stockings to her legs. The suspender's pimples snap as she fastens the stockings to her belt.

'What important . . . ?' You can hear you are a little grizzling child tossing in the bed, you can't help it.

Feet soft without shoes, she comes across and sits on the edge. The pale light from one window behind does not light her face. She is looking straight into your half-open eyes. You know your lids are gummy, lashes sticky with sleep. She is looking at everything ugly in her thick-skinned child.

The hand starts trying out what she has to say. 'You must be sensible, darling, understand why I must go back. Be of use. I don't think Papa would have married me if he had thought I was a *useless woman*. Now he would want me to do this. To go back and nurse the sick. The wounded—to go back to Egypt. It's all I can offer.' Her hand becoming hard. 'Do you see?'

Yes. She had her nursing diploma.

'Darling?'

Wouldn't want Mamma to stick a needle into my bottom when she is angry.

'Yes.' It sounds like 'esss'—silly little baby teeth falling out on the sheet, it is what she wants.

'I knew darling, you would see.'

She gets up, and goes back towards the window, her stockinged feet thumping across the gritty carpet, offering her face to the light from the window, Mamma no longer has the advantage.

'When are you going?'

She has these lines down her face. Like the ventriloquist's doll at the Zappeion.

'Well, soon—at once—because they have offered me return passage in this boat. I can't lose the opportunity, can I? To go back to where I am needed.' The way she swallows on what she is saying.

'Aunt Alison will come to fetch me—Take me to the boat. Alison will always be here—and kind Mrs Bulpit. You will not be alone.' She is staring at the light as it was on the window, or the curve of a branch knocking on the glass—or nothing. 'And soon we shall be together again.'

• • •

For the time being everyone seemed to have forgotten about her though Mrs Bulpit offered a bowl of what she called 'porridge.' It was as convenient to forget as it was to be forgotten. The house was buzzing with the thoughts and actions of those separately in it. As she went outside leaving Mamma to tissues and the bathroom, Mrs Bulpit was attacking the kitchen. Her gloves had changed from asbestos to rubber, her curls hidden in a scarf, the ears of which trembled as she scrubbed, poked, and sang. She had just finished *Two Sleepy People*, and was starting on *Red Sails in the Sunset.*

Light lay heavy—it made the paths look substantial where the concrete had not crumbled, tree trunks and the branches of trees had knotted like the muscles in men's bodies. Wherever rust had broken out it glowered like blood in the act of drying.

At a moment when they least expected each other the boy came down into the yard. Perhaps for this reason the half-rotten terrible steps ahead threw him and the things in the half-empty case he was carrying rattled round inside it.

He was forced by the situation to grunt something about '. . . school . . .'

'Mmh . . .?' she answered.

'When you commin?' There was menace in his voice, forced on him by school or the light or Australia or something.

'I haven't been told,' she replied with as much precision as she could muster.

She took a sideways look at the blond legs but could not face the pale blue eyes.

Though it wasn't called for, she informed him, 'My aunt—Mrs Lockhart—is coming for my mother.'

He muttered again, something about 'Bruce and Kevin . . .' to convey contempt, before turning his back. As he mounted the slope to reach the street he was grinding his soles into the concrete. His socks were down around his ankles. She knew enough to sense he was wearing them that way deliberately.

He had scarcely gone when she ran back quickly inside. Mrs Bulpit had started on *Yours*. It seemed quite natural that Mrs Bulpit and Mamma should be so irrelevant, not in control of the house. What she most feared, that Gilbert Horsfall might dispute her ownership, no longer troubled her. Certainly he was temporarily absent; but his presence would not have mattered now that she felt mastery was within her reach.

Skipping, almost, inside the room where he had spent the night, and which still had the smell of what she supposed was a boy's sleep, she did not even bother to glance at the warrant-officer's blown-up portrait. That too was irrelevant. She only slightly hesitated before approaching the chest-of-drawers with the dried-out wishbone of some large bird, goose or turkey, lying where she had noticed it the night before. With a confidence she would have found odious in anyone else, she hummed a little of the tune the woman was singing in the kitchen. She gave her imitation a tinny edge reaching a crescendo as she dragged on the sticky knob of that same upper drawer. Again it shot out and hit her where women don't like to be hit. There she had the advantage even over Mamma, even over boys, who might hit but can't hurt if you are strong. And she felt strong. She felt her thoughts were leaner than Gilbert Horsfall's. Inside the drawer the same tangle of used string, the roughed up dirty handkerchief lying on top of the laundered ones. She held her breath then slid her hand under the clean handkerchiefs, where women hide the valuables Turks and brigands are looking for, and precious secrets like love letters. Some of the letters had made her feel guilty. The jewels she had slipped on her fingers and round her neck, her flesh growing inside them. She had felt silly finally.

Now, under Gilbert Horsfall's handkerchiefs she came across the secret he had hidden. It was a jewel, rather a lumpy one, golden in colour, set in a brooch. Was it valuable? Had he stolen it? She shoved it back in its hiding place. She slammed the drawer. She might have reached the peak of power over this pale, threatening boy.

She did a few twirls in the centre of the room stretching out her plait as far as it would reach. Dropped the plait. Would it make her look foreign in Australia? It ought not to matter, now that she was strong—if she was. Mamma was leaving, the boy would return when school was out.

His used bed was still unmade. It looked very narrow against the wall. She shuffled towards and lay down on it raising her arms above her head in defiance of the bed's rightful owner. The mattress was thin and hard. She whimpered slightly, before turning on her side, taking the shape Mamma had rejected the night before. She lay listening. Now that Mrs Bulpit had shut up, she could hear her own heart jumping round inside her like a caught fish. Otherwise silence. She had the day to fill. She did not fit in. She lay snuffling, whimpering, rubbing her cheek against the single cold pillow to warm them both.

Hid yourself most of the day. Mamma did not call or come to look. If Mrs Bulpit called she soon gave up, too intent on all she suffered: '. . . from morning to night—in Australia, madam.' For the benefit of anyone interested, she announced, 'We only ever serve a light lunch.' She might have been talking to the air. Till Aunt Alison came.

'Oh yes, Mrs Lockhart, Madame Sklavos is in the lounge room. The little lass. I-reenee? Your auntie! A little bit upset—and entitled to it—under the circs . . .'

No-one followed up this initial concern by coming in search of the 'little lass.' It left you free to investigate Mrs Lockhart—you could hardly think of her as aunt—by more satisfactory methods than those which adults use for children. Sisterly voices were already issuing by bursts and gusts out of the *saloni* window round the corner. Vines and a thicket of shrubs provided perfect cover for a listener if one of the sisters should look out the window.

Mrs Lockhart had an older, throatier, smokier voice than Mamma's. 'Good Lord . . . meeting after all these years makes you feel bloody idiotic.'

'. . . unnatural . . .' Mamma corrected in her more precise and foreign-sounding voice from years spent in making foreigners understand, whereas Aunt Alison swallowed her words or bit them off like thread after it had served its purpose. Miss Adams would have found it slovenly speech.

'. . . always a bombshell artist, Gerry, but never let off one like this . . .' trumpets of smoke accompanied the Lockhart voice through the window.

'How a bombshell to want to bring my child to safety? I am letting off nothing. A situation forced on me by fate.'

'. . . like marrying that Greek commo—if you did—Harold bets you didn't—not that it matters—I'd never blame anybody for not—if it wasn't for the poor bastards of children . . .'

A cigarette butt came flinging out the window to smoulder on a mattress of damp leaves.

Mamma's voice had never sounded so cold and pure.

'We married to baptise the child. Whatever a Greek believes or doesn't believe in, birth and death are reasons for Orthodoxy.'

'All very high-flown, the Orthodoxy bit. In between, the drudgery was left to you.'

'Petros loved—he adored his child. But had to be away most of the time.'

Couldn't help hating this aunt's smoky voice. When Papa loved. *Adored.* Fingers spilling seed from these little pods which fringe the sill do not hurt what they sow. If you could only hurt this hurtful Lockhart voice, bite it out from where the words came hurtling.

'. . . away when you changed the nappy and powdered the rash in her little crotch.'

'Petros was dedicated to a cause . . .'

'Handy enough.'

'. . . which I married into. Something that you, Ally, could never understand, living in a country which has always been causeless.'

'I like to think we have a sense of duty towards our children.'

'Would I have brought her here if I hadn't felt it my duty?'

'And do you love her, too?'

'What an inquisition! Of course I—love—her.'

Mamma's fury is so fierce you can almost feel it burning from the other side of the sill. But do you, oh, Mamma, do you?

'Do you, I wonder?' Mrs Lockhart asks of anyone who has the answer. 'No-one ever went off at such a bat after dumping her dumpling.'

'The passage, I tell you—could I—in these days—refuse the offer?'

Mamma is really suffering. She is suffering, has always suffered from anything she suffers. The lies people tell make her suffer, but she suffers most when she tells her own.

'That was up to you—and the cause, I expect.' The Lockhart voice is sucking on another cigarette.

What you can't see is hard to believe. To see is always better than to hear. If only to see them at it. There is this flowerpot lying collecting snails under the skirt of the sooty vine. Turned wrongside up you will have a footstool from which, if careful, you can see inside the room, from the back of the sill.

Mamma's sister looks old, older it seems than Great Aunt Cleone Tipaldou, from being too much in the sun like the peasants. Her skin is rough as bark, scaly as a hen's legs. Mamma's brown eyes, capable of keeping her own secrets are not related to this blue, accusing Lockhart stare blazing out of the burnt face, skin shrivelled most noticeably where it forks below the throat and sweeps away inside any old kind of crumpled cotton frock. Mountain slopes crack open like this at the height of summer. Above the cleavage she is wearing a blackhead like a brooch. Would love to give Aunt Ally's blackhead a squeeze.

She is stamping, and if smoke and drought had allowed her, would have been shouting at the top of her voice about what they had got on to '—expect there's a man involved in it. You never ran out of men Gerry . . .'

Anger and argument have filled the room with movement. Mamma consoling her smooth arms avoids her stamping sister. Mamma moves very beautifully.

'I can't deny someone is taking an interest. It would be hypocritical wouldn't it?'

(Would it?) Mamma's eyes are as terrible in their own brown way as the accusing blue.

'. . . and Aleko was Petros' closest friend . . .'

'. . . and the Cause plays at shuttle-cock . . .'

They are going on at a great rate about principles. Neither understands the other. Perhaps in the end, nobody *understands*.

The Lockhart is clutching her long carton of American cigarettes as though her life depends on them.

'Well, Ireen can depend on me. Couldn't have her in my own house . . . four boys—and Harold didn't want to risk a girl—says he knows all about them. I reckon he must . . .'

Mrs Lockhart's skin is every moment shabbier while Mamma's arms and cheekbones, her beautiful neck look waxed. Why are you not in bed, Eirinitsa? Mamma is crying as you stand in the door like a wax figure, eyes closed, leaving anger and discipline to Papa. You could feel Papa hated you, for that moment, anyway. Will Aleko, his closest friend, hate too if he catches you staring at the wax figures? Or because you aren't his, will he leave it to Mamma to command? Only it will not happen, you will not be there, you . . .

The old cracked flowerpot slanting lurching cracking crunching you are standing in the slush and smell the quivering of mashed snails mercifully below the sill. There is the garden. *Doxa sto Theo*, there will always be the garden to scuttle through like any of its insects who have learnt the hiding places.

Scuttle then.

Looking back from where you have dropped on your knees on something sharp it no longer matters worse blood could not be drawn the sisters have arrived at the window and stand looking out a fright or at least suspicion has shut them up for the present they stand in the wreckage of their principles there is nothing they can see exactly except looking down the rubble of an old flowerpot their faces quivering like a pulp of drying snails. Almost as though they have been caught out like children.

The Lockhart glances at her wrist. 'Mustn't forget this boat you have to catch.' It is a relief to remember there is something she can do, where she can be of use, after straying into the prickly thicket of principles.

Mamma receives less comfort. '. . . yes, the boat . . .' She ought to feel released, perhaps she will when they draw up the gangway, but standing at the window, her ideals are still squirming for the trampling they have undergone in what she sees as this rough neglected Australian garden. She says screwing up her face, 'I must say good-bye to my poor child. I could not bear to have her come to the boat. That would be too heartrending.'

The Lockhart tears a fresh pack from the cellophane binding it to the carton. 'I don't doubt . . .' she turns a laugh into a cough, swivelling the end of a scaly nose.

Mamma says, 'It is only a temporary separation. When we have won, Eirene will come . . . join in building a better Greece . . .'

They turn back into the house, two sisters united over practical details, like stuffing a suitcase with what has almost been forgotten, and fastening the hasps.

Mamma's voice is choked at first. When it is next heard, agape now, she is standing on the rotten back steps. She clears her throat and the voice floats out as clear as that of a singer in opera. 'Eirene? We must say good-bye darling. Mamma cannot miss her boat.'

The Lockhart one has gone up the path to start the car.

Mamma continues, her voice like a descending scale of feathers floating down through the tangle of trees, as you lie with your face in rotting leaves, so warm and smoky they may be at the point of kindling. A red centipede is crawling over your bare arm. A black beetle scratches at your cheek as it tries to climb.

Presently the guardian's voice. '. . . too upset I expect, Madame Sklavos. Poor little soul.' She blunders about a bit, because it is her duty, barely leaving the path once she has run her face into a great spider's web '. . . urrh . . . nasty! Poison a person . . .'

'Sensitive child . . . don't you worry, madam, every care will be taken of her. Mamma and the woman are struggling up the path towards the snorting car carrying Mamma's heavy suitcase. Mamma soon leaves it to the one whose services will be paid for.

Soon there will be the garden alone. If only you could take the form of this red thread of a centipede or beetle that might have crawled out of the dregs of an inkwell to claw and scratch and burrow and hide amongst what is not just rottenness but change to change. To become part of this thick infested garden so swallowed up where Mamma suffers. You could no longer want either house or garden for your own. Only to burrow. Only this other enemy would come, and crush the beetle out of you. Crush you as a girl too, if you did not resist.

As you get up on your uncomfortable heels, the garden which is yours, in your nostrils and under your nails, glooms and shimmers with whatever is to happen. The gate squeals—is it Gilbert Horsfall, socks around his ankles, the battered case with very little joggling round inside it, returning to dispute your ownership?

Ready yourself to kick him in the shins when the pins and needles have died like so many insects in what are still your legs.

Mrs Bulpit had given up clambering up and down the paths and steps of a garden she would not have wanted to own, if it hadn't gone with the house Reg bought.

'When you've stopped being contrary, young lady,' she called at her last gasp, 'you can show yourself and we'll come to terms.'

She went inside banging the door with the hole in the mosquito wire.

Presently the boy came out, chewing on a hunk of bread. He was carrying a second, holding it at a distance from him. Though the evening had started cooling off, the fat from this second slice of bread had begun to melt, he could feel it messing up his fingers as the dripping from the hunk he was tucking into had smeared his mouth, fattening his lips, making them lazy and content.

If he didn't find her, he could eat hers as well, so he meandered on, not particularly looking, at moments forgetting the mission Ma Bulpit had sent him on. Then he caught sight of this Irene Sklavos standing below him at the sea wall, which was where he would have least liked to find her. He was looking down on that straight white parting as she scraped the gulls' white scribble from the wall.

'Hi,' he mumped, but not loud enough, he really didn't want to find her.

She went on scraping, and he went on, his thick-soled school shoes growing heavier as he dragged them along the gritty path to show his indifference, and yet not loud enough for her to hear. If only he would never reach her. What ever would he say to this foreign girl if he did?

As he made the last elbow in the downward path, brushing up against the guava tree to remain unseen till the moment they must face each other, he turned in the direction of the city, and that evening dazzle of sun and water. There was no postponing it. She jerked round to see who had caught her out—or was she catching him? Her eyes were still screwed up in her face, either dazzled, or disgusted.

'She sent you this,' he mumbled.

'What is it?'

'Bread and dripping.'

She took hold of it at last as though it might have been a dog's turd you were handing her.

Squinting at it. 'I never ate anything like this.' Smelling, touching the stuff with the tip of her tongue, biting in.

'Aah—po po po!' Spitting, but not throwing it away.

'. . . love it . . .' Chewing his last rag of crust he made the act look as ugly as he could. 'If you don't want it you can give it here.'

She became more screwed up than ever, and disgusted or something, before glancing back over her shoulder at the fire in the west. 'My mother's sailing.'

'Didn't go to see her off.'

'I wouldn't be here if I had, would I?'

He felt himself grow so hot and red she could only notice. He hated her for the weakness she provoked. She must be one of those, not girls, he hadn't known enough of them, but like grown-up people, fathers, teachers, who go out of their way to make you look stupid—when you weren't—or were you? He swallowed down the last of the mush his crust had become.

'I wouldn't go. I didn't want to.' She suddenly began biting into the bread and dripping.

'I'd go along any time to watch a ship sail.'

'You wouldn't understand, even if I told you.' The bread was making knots in her throat as it went down. She looked to him like that emu in the zoo, a skinny black emu.

'All right,' he said. 'You're too clever by half. Anybody can see that.'

She might have been going to cry only the bread and dripping had stopped her mouth up. She was settling down. She was wiping her fingers on the stone wall. A stillness they were sharing made him feel more friendly towards her.

Again she was looking out, across the water, but not in the direction of the blazing city.

'Where I live,' she said very slowly, 'there's an island with a volcano on it and a temple. You can see the island across the gulf.'

'What, a real volcano?'

'Of course, but dead for centuries though no volcano's ever extinct—it's only waiting,' she blubbed or shouted, 'for the next time.'

He would have liked to get away from this dark snake of a girl.

They were leaving the water. They had begun mounting the path which wound upward through the garden. Antipathy could have died, as an ashy cloud was to obscure the fire in the west, and violence had been suppressed centuries before in the volcano only one of them had seen.

'Did you ever go to the island?' he asked.

'No,' she said dully. 'There was always too much to do. My father and mother were political. There was no-one to take me. My father died in prison then the war came.'

'How did he die?' the boy asked.

'We don't know.'

She announced it with a flatness which sounded odd. The violence of that extinct volcano was still stirring and bubbling in him. There was something about this volcano which impressed him more deeply than bombs and war; the volcano was more private, secret.

Perhaps because she had seen it, if only at a distance, the girl was less impressed by it. Her father died in prison. Was the father someone the Colonel would disapprove of? As you disapproved of Irene Sklavos. He shivered as a pittosporum scratched him and recoiled on to her thin black arm.

She did not seem to notice he had touched her, perhaps thinking of the mother who was leaving her behind.

'What was this temple on the island?' he asked, quietly so as not to disturb a situation which had grown quite agreeable.

'People used to go there to pray to the goddess.'

They continued trudging up the broken path.

'Do you pray?' he asked more carefully than ever.

'Mm?' she sighed. 'It depends.'

Remembering his experience of communal prayer with the Ballards, he said flat out 'I don't—not any more than I have to.' His mother was such a vague figure he could barely remember what she would have thought. The Colonel was not a church goer while expecting his son to do his duty. 'Do your parents pray?' he asked the girl.

'Papa was a Marxist. But I think he prayed when things got bad. Mamma says religion isn't rational.'

'If your parents were Marxist—rationalist—all that—what do you know about praying then?'

'Aunt Cleonaki taught me—about the Panayia and the Saints. Some of the saints are good,' she giggled, 'but you mustn't believe all of it, Aunt Cleone says, that's pagan superstition.'

His breath was coming in short gasps. It wasn't just from the cliff they were climbing by stages. He wanted her to continue talking. 'What's this Pana-year?'

'The Mother of God. She's lovely. When I pray at all I pray to her.'

They were drifting dreamily together, through a gathering dusk which the tangle of garden intensified.

'There's the *pneuma* too. I like to think about it.'

'What's the *pneuma*?' His breath was almost snorting, it had grown so heavy.

'I don't know.' She conceded to herself. 'I can't tell you—not in English.'

He believed she was lying. She would always try to put one over him.

To show that he hadn't been led away he assumed the voice the Lockharts—Bruce and Kevin—might have used.

'Wonder what the old girl's got for tea.'

She said she wasn't hungry.

He told her, 'I could put away twice the muck we'll get.'

He did not seem to have impressed her. They were on the lap before the last flight of stone steps. They were passing the broken statue, under the largest, darkest fig with the flying air roots, where they had first met. Her silence made his skin creep as if ants were walking over it. Was she still thinking of the Panayear and the *pneuma*? A milky cloud was floating overhead in a gap between the branches of the great fig.

As they came out into the yard he began clattering his boots against the concrete as though to rid them of accumulated dirt blaring a non-tune from behind large bared teeth. She followed him meekly. Any conversation they might have had was buried inside them.

Inside the house you get away from Gilbert Horsfall as quickly as you can. You have said all you had to say to him. You wish he wasn't living here. From sounds in the kitchen the guardian probably won't cause immediate trouble. You make for the bedroom where in spite of Mamma, you had been most nearly private. Your few things must be there unpacked from the suitcase Mamma has taken back with her.

Your things are there, higgledy piggledy on a chair, and overflowing on to the floor. A stocking hanging from the chair arm, might never have belonged to anybody. The room has already changed back to what it must have been before strangers were admitted. You feel trapped beneath a great white canopy or mosquito net. Though the bed is not at the centre of the room, it and the invisible net will swim centre for sleep and dreams where there were a few stray hairpins and a sprinkling of face powder on the dressing table the night before, a photo of the husband has appeared, a smaller duplicate print of the one in the room where Gilbert sleeps. (What would you do with a husband, not a warrant officer but one say like Papa angrily poised above Mamma's wax figure? You could always keep your eyes shut.) Too many traps. During the day the carpet has sprouted a thick mossy pile. As you advance towards the dressing table your feet scarcely move. It might suck you under, to become a corpse along with other insects it has snared.

Apart from the upright photograph the most noticeable object on the dressing table you might never reach is the box from which the owner's powder must have spilled before she whisked it away. Printed, or you could say written on the lid of the box again in its rightful place, were the words *Mon Desir*. Inside the box, half open from recent slapdash use is the puff, the powder in its shabby swansdown clotted with moisture. Looking at it makes you sneeze. You could see the puff coating its owner's marzipan flesh with a tint deeper than was natural.

The worst trap of all is the thought of sharing the bed with Mrs Bulpit as you had to some extent shared it with Mamma. Mrs B's suspender belt snapping must sound like the crack of a whip. In her dreams of the warrant officer she might roll over and flatten even a sleepless partner.

Escape immediately if the net, if the moss in which you stand rooted amongst insect corpses, allowed. There is this sound of metal rings. Are they those of the net canopy, rustling into action? Extraordinarily the moss is withering, parting like the Egyptian sea. I may fall as I shoot towards the door on a floor as glassy as one on which they scatter powder for those who have learnt to dance.

It is the woman's voice rustling out of the kitchen deeper in the house, from out of cutlery and pans, and the smell of onion, no longer the sickly scent of *Mon Desir*. '. . . Show her, Gilbert, now that you've found her, where to wash her hands, I don't want to see either of you till I have your tea ready. There's no room for moping or muttering children. Other people have their troubles, you know. One of my migraines is coming on. So if it isn't too much to ask . . . I'll be obliged if you behave reasonably . . .'

The voice sounded slurred, whether from the migraine or something she had taken for it. She was obviously under the weather, which was not surprising, Eirene felt.

If it had not been for the positive smell of frying onion you might have broken down and cried in this dark passage on the way from the bedroom to nowhere.

Suddenly the boy appeared, whom she had dismissed a short while before. She was glad to see his face glimmer at her, still formless as it approached.

'Come on,' he said, 'you don't have to wash if you don't feel like it. Turn the tap on, rattle round in the sink a bit, and she'll calm down.'

He led her out to a scullery or laundry which overlooked part of the back yard. Here he began behaving as he had advised. But Eirene chose to fill the sink and cool her hands. These looked surprisingly helpless for one who normally recognised her own powers. As she wrapped them together and round a piece of yellow soap, and allowed them to escape from her, the hands became a pair of fish too small to send to the market. Which did not remove the probability that somebody would eat them, and in the scullery the smells of sick linoleum and the yellow soap now stranded shiny on the drying board took over from the comforting stench of frying onion.

'There's a towel,' he told her, 'but too wet to use. Seeing you were silly enough to wash, you'd better dry your hands on yourself.'

She was glad to come across this practical strain in her companion. She might make use of it later on. In the morning it filled some of the emptiness left by her mother's going away.

After the washing ceremony they went outside for no definite purpose beyond passing the time till their tea was ready. They sat on the steps leading to the yard. The dark trees and browned-out lights of the city beyond encouraged a melancholy which she suspected the boy did not share. His body was harder. It helped him not to mind things so much.

He sat scratching a scab on his knee, and from the goo he felt under his fingers must have got it off finally. He smeared the blood about on the skin but it gave him no idea how he might impress this girl, who had seen a volcano, whose father had died in prison and who had come from where a war was taking place.

'Did you see anybody killed?' he asked, 'in the war, I mean.'

'No,' she said. 'The war was in the mountains. It was at this time still . . . heroic.' She spoke with such slow and special emphasis he could see it rounding in the dark in front of them, like a drop of suspended blood transformed into a jewel. 'Oh, I did see something,' she remembered. 'An old man hit by a tank outside the gardens. His head was squashed. His brains were mashed into the paving. They said it was done by a British tank. Because the British were in retreat, you see. Then the Germans marched in—and that was different. British MTV took us off because we were friends.'

He envied her all she had experienced and her professional use of terms. It was too unfair that he had so little to offer.

'Were you afraid?'

'Not really. I was taken care of. It didn't seem to be happening to me. It would have been different if we had stayed for Greece. I planned to take Evthymia's sharpest meat knife and kill a German on a dark night.'

'Doesn't sound to me as bad as the Blitz in London.'

'I don't know about that,' she said.

'Thousands killed every night the bombers came over. It was one big firework display. When you got used to it you didn't stay in the shelters with a mob of people smelling and farting. Bombs tore through the shelters, anyway. You got used to walking through the streets through the shrapnel. And in the ruins by day. One night I was shot out of the corridor on my mattress—landed in the street—thought I was dead till I heard a warden ask, 'Anyone know this boy's name?' Somebody did. They said, 'It's Nigel Horsfall from a block away.'

'I thought your name was Gilbert.'

'Yes,' he said, 'it is.'

They continued sitting side by side on the steps overlooking the garden. Had she dropped to him? From her dreamy look he didn't think so. And he wasn't that much a liar. Though he had been evacuated with those other kids before the bombs began to fall you knew what it was like as though you had been there, from what you had been told. If you had imagination you knew. And some had died with poor old Nigel, his only friend. You knew through Nigel. Silly of you though to let the name slip.

But she hadn't cottoned on. He took another look. He might have taken her by the hand. They were wandering through the blacked-out streets. In the ruin of some great house they looked down at the marble face, like of some goddess broken out of a volcanic temple, only the lips began to breathe, very gently. Irene Sklavos did not seem surprised, it could have been her own face whitened. There was a man and woman pressed up against each other in a gateway. Nigel Brown who knew more about it said they were fucking. Irene Sklavos seemed unsurprised, when you—or was it Nigel?—led her farther into these desolated streets which belonged to you both by rights of the life you had begun to share, through imagination and dreams.

He looked at her again to see what she was thinking, from her side-on face. If he had pulled her round and stared at her eye to eye, she would have had the round, gently breathing face of the yellow, bomber's moon. Side-on, she was this sharp know-all. If he had touched her elbows or knee-caps they would have been as sharp, as cutting as the words of teachers in class or the Lockhart louts—Kevin and Bruce. He couldn't tell which side she was on.

When they were seated one each side of her at the kitchen table their guardian told them, 'You may wonder at us eating such a nice piece of steak in wartime. It's because Mr Strutt did me a favour—a mate of Reg's—another of us from the Old Country—always down at the Imperial when we was running it—all returned men—things was different in those days.'

She had cut up her steak very fine. She was only messing with it, the chips were more to her taste. She gobbled at them in between what she had to tell. One of the big flabby chips fell out of her mouth and landed in the gravy, which shot up and spotted her dress.

'You children,' she said, 'wouldn't understand.'

Then she realised she ought to clean up the gravy spots and began mopping at them with a hankie. Her red lip-stuff had worn off. Her mouth should have looked normal, except most grown-ups never look that.

Gilbert Horsfall looked across at Irene Sklavos. They should have felt good for a giggle, but they weren't. Like Ma Bulpit, the girl was only picking at her food. She had the sniffles. She looked darker than ever, if not positively green.

In between observing the others and disapproving their wasted opportunities, Gilbert Horsfall polished off his own plateful. He still felt hungry. He might have helped out, he thought—urgh, no, not the mess Ma Bulpit's shiny teeth had refused, now sitting in its own fat. But Irene had hardly touched her tea. He could imagine taking a mouthful of the untouched steak and converting the stringy old stuff into a delicious tenderness. He shivered as his teeth entered the soft, greasy chips. All his imagined acts were becoming so real, he wondered whether Irene would see that he was almost peeing himself. But she kept her eyelids lowered.

Ma Bulpit had begun pulling out. 'Expect you're waiting on the pudding,' she mumbled. 'All young things have a sweet tooth,' chair grating almost to toppling, 'that's why we lose them,' as she stumbled in the direction of the kitchen which swallowed her signature tune. 'In the old days I was famous for my Apple Betty.'

Irene Sklavos raised her eyelids.

'What is this Betty?'

Her question promoted Gilbert Horsfall to the rank of friend. He was both grateful for the honour and reluctant to accept it.

'Arr,' he said, sticking out his lips remembering his Lockhart mentors, 'it's got these sort of pip-scales in it that make you wanter puke—right enough if you've still got to fill your belly.'

She looked so unhappy he clenched his knuckles under the table. He hoped she wouldn't take him for a Lockhart, but could think of no way of showing her he was otherwise.

Aluminium began battering the silence which had gathered in the kitchen.

Mrs Bulpit appeared leaning in the doorway. 'Got a bit burnt,' she explained, 'on the top.'

The accident didn't prevent laughter spilling out from around her teeth. She could even have been feeling relieved, anyway for a moment, because in aiming at, and plummeting into her chair, she declaimed, '. . . you gotter forgive . . . me migraine's coming on . . . a martyr to it.'

She sat holding a hand above her eyes, like a vast white celluloid shade, while her audience wondered whether they were impressed or suspicious.

Suddenly removing the shade from her afflicted eyes, she announced, 'It's the migraine that's kept me from turning out the lovely room I have for our little lass. Too much happening at once,' she sighed. 'I'll get round to it, but tonight she'll have to camp somewhere else.'

Eirene Sklavos sat very upright, her neck grown as thin as the stem of a flower. The lobes of her ears seemed to flicker like freshly opened peablossom, only that was impossible. It was more likely that her earlier suspicion would be confirmed, and that she would have to share Mrs Bulpit's bed.

'Aren't we going to get the pud, Mrs Bulpit?' Gilbert Horsfall thought it reasonable to ask.

She was too preoccupied to answer.

And Eirene thought him stupid not to recognise the direction from which serious threats can be expected. In spite of his male strength, he would remain an unreliable ally.

The Bulpit was starting again. 'What I think I'll do,' she mumbled as she unlocked her thighs gripping the chair arms with her great white squelchy hands, 'I'll make up the other bed in Reg's—in Mr Bulpit's room—till we get ourselves sorted out.'

She sounded as though she was addressing herself—or the former W/O—rather than those more deeply concerned. Of these, Eirene might have felt relief, Gilbert Horsfall could have been stunned, but neither of them revealed a reaction, which in any case their guardian was prepared to ignore.

As she rolled once again out of her constricting chair, she appeared more than anything relieved to have made what amounted to a decision. '. . . and I wouldn't call it a bad one . . .' She continued mumbling as she moved about in different dark recesses of the house '. . . the best I can manage to suit us all' her voice additionally blurred and furry from the smells of damp and mothballs she was dragging out of cupboards.

At one stage passing through the room in which the less important actors in the play had continued sitting, herself a blanketed monument with a train of sheet attached, she suggested, 'If you two kids thought of getting on with the washing up, a person would be much obliged.'

Gilbert Horsfall grimaced, winked, and went through a series of wriggly motions with his torso. In normal circumstances it might have amused his audience. Now Eirene Sklavos could only accept his leadership and follow him dully into the kitchen.

There at least it was warm, not to say fuzzy from the charred ruin of the pudding in its aluminium dish, the remains of congealed steak and chips, and what must have been brandy fumes, judging from a half-emptied bottle standing beside the sink in important isolation.

Gilbert grabbed it and reeled as he thrust it at Eirene. ''Ave a swig?' he croaked.

She ducked away. But some of the brandy splashed over her.

Gilbert actually stuck the mouth of the bottle in his and she thought she heard a glug or two and saw his throat in motion. She couldn't be sure. She couldn't be sure of anything about this boy. But for the moment she depended on him. For that reason she even loved him, she thought.

Removing the bottle from his lips, he gasped, 'So much for the orgy. Now it's down to business.'

He was filling the sink, swizzling the water with soap imprisoned in a wire basket scraping plates into an already smelly bin.

She would have liked to help, but didn't know how. In their Marxist household there had been Vaso, with her *arthritika*, in Aunt Cleone's vaguely democratic Republican establishment there was Evthymia to attend to duties beneath a lady. Without slaves, Eirene

Sklavos pricked her finger on a fork before throwing that weapon into the sinkful of frothing water.

She stood looking at the pinpoint of blood on the cushion of her finger. It provided some kind of focus point.

'Here, dreamy. Take the towel, if you're too grand to dirty your hands.'

She obeyed him rather gratefully, and began rubbing at the cutlery and plates, but the towel only seemed to make them wetter. It did not matter. Nothing did. While Mamma was sitting in the saloon, listening to men express their ideas. Particularly those of Father's friend Aleko. Mamma grew still watching the little black tufts of hair on the backs of Aleko's fingers.

Gilbert Horsfall's hands were blond, shiny, hairless as he plunged and re-plunged them in the sink. They were scarcely human.

'Do you like doing it?' she murmured.

'Do I *like*?' as he flipped his hands he flicked back water into the sink. 'You gotter do it here. Australians are supposed to be useful.'

'We didn't have to. So I never learned.'

'Thought your people were supposed to be commos.'

'They had their ideas. There was always someone, someone else to do the things like washing up.'

'I wouldn't do any bloody washing up if you didn't have to stay on the right side of the old girl.'

Across the distance separating them they stood looking at the charred ruin of the Apple Betty. Nothing had ever looked so extinct.

Gilbert Horsfall grabbed a fork and stabbed at it. 'Bloody well burnt out!' he cried.

It made her giggle in spite of her deep melancholy.

'*Extinct*—like that Greek volcano you were telling me about.'

The charred pudding, the volcano, reminded them of more important matters, for they began drifting by common though silent consent towards the exercise. Mrs Bulpit was commanding in what had been, was still in fact, the warrant officer's bedroom.

'There!' she exclaimed, staggering back from tucking in a stray end of sheet between the mattress and a narrow bed. 'Nobody could find fault with that.'

A veil of perspiration streamed over her suetty face as she stood admiring her handiwork. She looked quite religious.

Till snapping out of her trance, 'I think we'll agree to call it a day. Thanks for the washing-up, Gilbert—Ireen,' she leered as she lumbered out.

But popped back to remind, 'I hope you're not mischievous children. No *pillow-fights*!'

After that she could be heard in the kitchen extracting the pudding from its aluminium armour, and removing her mouth from a bottle, it sounded.

The children were left to face the details of an oppressive present and a frightening, larger-than-life future.

There was no tune to Gilbert's whistling as he tore himself out of his clothes. Eirene did not know what to do, say, or where to look. She continued standing beside what Mrs Bulpit had ordained as her bed. She did in fact slightly glance in her ally's direction. In his nakedness he had his back to her, buttocks tensed, ribs in each case visible. He was skinnier than she would have imagined. Then he began putting on these old pyjamas with stripes of washed-out blue on them, and tying a string round his middle.

He asked, 'Aren't you going to undress?' though still with his back to her.

'No,' she replied.

He got into bed, pulling the sheet over his head.

'We didn't last night, Mamma and I.'

'You'll be smelly if you don't, two nights running.'

She took off her shoes and stood them together as neatly as Aunt Cleone would have demanded. She pulled off her stockings, rolling each into a ball before sticking them in her empty shoes. She too took off her dress, folded and hung it over the foot of the bed. After this there was nothing to prevent her getting between Mrs Bulpit's damp grey sheets.

She should have felt safely sandwiched, and the surrounding silence saved her from further depredations, if it had not been for a distant crash.

'What is it—Gilbert?' she asked.

'Possums.' His mouth made a big round O through the sheet.

'They must be huge.'

'Some of them are,' the sheet veiling his face quivered with suppressed sniggers, before he snatched it off.

'Gotter turn the light out!'

He tore across the room in the washed-out pyjamas, the legs and sleeves of which were by now too short.

Then darkness rushed at them. It swallowed the leaning warrant officer, the pieces of Bulpit furniture, and anything as personal as the hopes and fears of those temporarily living there.

A violent plunk of springs told Eirene Sklavos that Gilbert Horsfall must have landed back on his bed. The distance separating them stretched even wider than before. The rough sheets were sawing at her. The bloodspot on the finger she had pricked with a fork swelled against the darkness and swelled, becoming—

was it? The head of that old man a tank had crushed outside the Royal (or National) gardens. Swelling and spilling. The old man's bloody brains.

'Tell us something.'

Gilbert's voice had roughened in an attempt to become a man's. She recognised the tone. It was that of the men Mamma enjoyed talking to. Holding her head on one side. You tried out your head in imitation against the rough, damp, Bulpit pillow.

'I haven't anything,' she murmured back across the darkness lying between them.

'You had plenty when we were talking before.'

'That was then.' She heard herself mewing into the pillow.

'What's up?'

She couldn't tell him. She hardly knew.

The darkness was rocking, not so much the boat carrying her back to a war, but the motions of the dance she was dancing in the *patisserie* in Alexandria. Mamma hated this officer, but her body could not refuse to dance.

'You're a sooky sort of girl,' Gilbert Horsfall was complaining.

All the girls he had known were crowding in on her through the darkness, long-legged yellow-haired English girls, cold and perfect Miss Adams said she loved the daffies in spring time at Home. Some of Gilbert's girls wore lipstick. They were women in front.

'I can't help it,' she mewed worse than ever.

They entered the worst silence of all. Was any of it happening to them? The war, Australia, this vast Bulpit room with iron beds clamped to opposite walls.

'Why don't you come over?' he twittered.

Why should she? It made her raise her head against the pillow. Others always came to Mamma. This boy with the hoarse voice and shrunk pyjamas. Gilbert Horsfall's wriggly torso. Who knew about bread and dripping. She snorted slightly, licked her lips. She had never felt so tall and slender. Her strength was returning.

'Not if you're afraid,' he said, 'but you needn't worry about *her*. She's as safe as a lead sinker once she's under the brandy.'

'*I'm* not afraid. It's you. Otherwise you'd come over here.'

To demonstrate the truth of her remark and her own superiority, she jumped out of bed before he could, only regretting her recklessness halfway across the gritty darkness, and set up a mewing again on stubbing her toe on a castor. At once the dark was full of threats. It was a comfort to find herself thrown forward, sprawling like a crab on Gilbert Horsfall's bony chest.

'*Ahoo . . .* it's cold,' she moaned.

'Not where I come from,' he whinged back.

The temperature was at least an excuse for her to get into bed and pull up the clothes. She would have liked to snuggle, but lay as stiff and straight as he was lying. It seemed there was nothing either of them could do beyond go along with those private palpitations, fluctuating with rubbery persistence, and listen to each other's breathing.

In the distance there was the sound of a ship, the grumbling of a city's traffic, farther still the explosions and guns, the cries of those who are wounded, which your blood and your dreams know everything about.

After a while, when they slid into what felt like a shallow backwater, halfway between thoughts and sleep, he thumped his limbs against the mattress and started getting at her again, 'Tell me about the *pneuma*.'

'I told you, I can't. Not in English.'

'But you could if you wanted to.'

'You can't! You can't! It's the sort of thing you can't talk about.'

'If I was dying,' he croaked, twisting his head from side to side, grinding a feverish body against the mattress, 'you'd hold out on me?'

She could feel her teeth grow very small as she smiled at the darkness.

'It's like the moon.'

'The moon's pagan, isn't it?'

'Not always.' She was very happy to discover this.

'I bet you're not telling me anything of what you know.' In his expostulation and feverish tossing, his wrist brushed against hers. She was surprised to find it covered with minute hooks.

She would have liked her wrist to give into his but did not dare. Then again, she didn't want to, did she?

'Hadn't we better go to sleep?' she said, and turned her back on him.

She got a surly grunt.

Not long after she didn't know what had happened to Gilbert Horsfall. She was sitting by herself at the small round table its top moulded out of pig's brawn edged with a pie-crust in some kind of metal. Not by herself really there was the small white cup with its sludge of Turkish—no, Greek coffee, and the glass with the half-finished *Café Liegeois* (more than the solid glass and its half-drunk contents she was conscious of the voice which had ordered it.) Her own *consommation* was out of focus except as something sweet and sticky. Like your fingers. Mamma *hated* sticky fingers.

Now it was the music stickily revolving inside the oval of this *patisserie* that Mamma should have condemned. This *Cruel Tango*. Like a sticky drum revolving and revolving. Leaning forward chin in hand brought you closer to the dancers, stamping a point into the floor (brawn again). The thick ankles in wartime shoes, Mamma says it is impossible to look elegant in wartime, Maltese, Jewish, Greek, Armenian, Hungarians and Romanians are different, because professional, or dishonest. As she revolves, with the *axiomatikos* who has brought them to the *patisserie*. She can't resist the sticky dance any more than the old lady's *loulou* beside her on the gold chain can resist the strawberry tartlet served by the Arab on the surface of the pig's-brawn table.

As the dancers revolve to the repetitive music of the *Cruel Tango*, bump and stamp, the Greek, the Maltese, the Armenian, the thick ankles, the short-legged Jewesses, and more professional Romanians and Hungarians. Stamp and swerve. The pistachio eyes of some dancers. Eyes beaded with Egyptian flies. O *Cruel Tango*.

Mamma twists and turns in the arms of the Greek *axiomatikos*. His badly fitted uniform, particularly between the legs, Mamma is the one who cuts and thrusts. He is her dummy. Her lips wear something brittle in the cruel tango. For Papa who died? For the Greek cause? For herself? Never for you. The sticky tears rain down on the unfinished *consommation* in this cruel dream.

She awoke crying. Gilbert, too, must have been asleep. He felt hot and moist as they lay against each other, tumbled into the same heap. Now he started lashing about, perhaps to show he had been awake all the while. It was only she who had been a prey to dreams.

'What you were dreaming about. Was it bad?' he asked.

'Not really.' She paused, wondering how far her conscience, according to Aunt Cleone, would condone a lie. 'Actually,' she said, in her best Miss Adams voice, 'I was dreaming about the moon.'

'That old *pneuma* again!'

'No, the moon,' she corrected him firmly, as though the *pneuma* were her private property.

'Sometimes,' she conceded, 'if you pray hard enough—if you want *badly*—you can be drawn up inside it.'

'Were you—in this dream?'

'Yes.' She lay listening to her dishonest heart.

'And what about me?'

'Oh, you weren't in it—in any way—in the dream. I don't see why you should have been.'

They had restored the distance between them.

'Sometimes when the Blitz was on I used to draw the black-out curtains. I thought if I could see the bombs falling I'd know the best way to escape. But you never saw. Only the moon.'

The moon's blue, gelatinous face with the forms of those milky twins inside it.

Before falling asleep, before the act of levitation took place, they drifted together again, their unprotesting skins, inside the steamy envelope of Bulpit sheets.

Mrs Lockhart has driven up in this old brown dislocated car, maltreated by the kicks, the shoving, the protests of too many boys' feet and bodies. She has come to investigate the niece and take her to school. Perhaps a more difficult situation than any Mrs Lockhart has ever managed, though she is used to difficult situations, what with Harold and the boys. Harold doesn't drive. He takes the ferry to the Department. He has always considered his not driving a superior accomplishment. He refers to 'Alison's car', which would have made it hers even if she hadn't wanted it. Actually she has always wanted it. It is more her home than the equally maltreated, ricketty, weatherboard house in which they live.

Now she sits in her more personal, mobile home at the Bulpit's gate, pausing a moment in an inevitably active life, before making an actively distasteful move. If it were not for this she could have been enjoying her freedom, under a blue sky, in a blaze of winter sunshine. She has with her everything she most needs (her supply of cigarettes and tissues) and no appendages (of course she loves the boys, she is less sure of Harold—yes, she is very very uncertain that she should have fallen into such a trap as marriage with Harold). And now Gerry's child, Ally sighs. She swivels her dented, sunburnt nose. She sweeps the ash out of her cleavage (one bitch of a friend suggests she ought to see a dermatologist about this blackhead) and starts clambering out of the Chev. Can you be starting an early arthritis? Give Harold additional grounds for playing the absentee husband.

'Oh yes, Mrs Lockhart, the little lass is waiting for you.'

The dreadful Bulpit has assembled her charge early, only too glad to unload her on other unwilling hands. She is standing in the lounge room, picking at the arm of one of Mrs Bulpit's seedy chairs.

'Here's your auntie, love.'

The Bulpit ducks out too willingly.

The child does not look up. She continues picking. She is neater than anything Alison has ever envisaged. Alison experiences a spasm of revulsion from the contradictory details of Geraldine's complex life. The fact that they are sisters has always amazed her. This dark child is the most amazing fact of all.

'Well, Ireen . . .'

Should they kiss? At least Gerry was never a kisser. Never even seen her kiss a man. And the child obviously doesn't want to be mauled by a gratuitous aunt.

Better sit down a moment or two for decency's sake. Plunk on the Bulpit springs.

'I expect you find it all very strange . . .'

'esss.'

Oh Lord the lighter's given out. These bloody wartime flints. Lord—without my cigs. 'Do you think you could ask Mrs Bulpit for a box of matches?'

'esss.'

She trots out. The neat, the pretty are usually cunning—the type Harold takes up with. At least he saw the red light, without even meeting Ireen, and refused to have her at the house. Blamed it on the boys.

When it's Gerry really. Always was. Harold hadn't turned up by then. But always. At the dances. Whirling out in a waltz. Shoving away at a foxtrot, up against their crotches. They said your sister's stuck up but it never reduced her market value. Geraldine Pascoe. Became a nurse. I ask you. Never believed in Gerry's vocation for a moment. Lead them on and tie them down, erection and all, under a sheet that was it. No typing pool for Gerry. *Touch* typing—ha ha. Can't think why Harold ever. Perhaps he married a typist. Those boring novels nobody will ever publish.

I am plain, plain, plain. Mother said it. Father even called it ugly, the night of the great piss up, when he came, and went, and stayed away forever.

Here she is. Back with the matches. Tripping pretty sweeting. Who ever said it?

'Thank you, dear. It's sweet of you.' Hypocritical word, but what they use, 'That's better.' Cough, cough. Smoke, if you could tell her, or any one of any of those damn parsons, is one of the few remaining mysteries.

Instead cough. 'Your mother must be proud of you.'

The child turns on those eyes, not Gerry's could be the Greek commo's—or her own? God, yes, I hope they're her own—if it wouldn't make her lovelier.

'Ireen, dear—we're late enough—we ought to start for school—hope it won't be too shocking—it won't—the boys love it . . .'

Oh God, she's still looking at me.

'If there's ever anything you need, dear, or want to know—you'll ask me, won't you?'

'Yes, Mrs Lockhart.'

Oh God. Well I *am*, aren't I?

'Where's Mrs Bulpit? We're going! Mrs Bul-pit? On our *wayhheh*!'

She comes running, the ghastly creature, head first, almost over the lounge.

'The lunch,' she gobbles. 'A child needs a nourishing cut lunch—specially in wartime.'

Not a bad old stick, she's even produced a case.

'Old, but it'll serve, Mrs Lockhart, till we get something better.'

Ireen takes the battered case. She holds it at the end of a stiff arm. It might have contained a bomb instead of this other jumping object—a cut lunch.

You didn't want any sort of lunch, least of all a cut one. *They* cut Vasieolis' throat. If you stopped eating, you would die quietly, painlessly. They will pick you up like a bunch of wilted spinach, from which the green will have drained away. No blood, either green or red.

Anyway, for this moment, you would have liked to live in such a way, following the Australian aunt up the path through the garden to which you no longer have or want to have a right. Belonging nowhere. The cat tripping across ahead her tail in the air belongs somewhere here, in this garden which you believed was becoming yours.

The aunt has wrinkles in her skirt below her behind. Wrinkles in her stockings. She is what Aunt Cleone calls *basse classe*. Mamma sees poverty as a virtue. Class is a different matter. Here Mamma would agree with Aunt Cleone even when her own sister is at stake. But Alison Lockhart is scarcely Mamma's sister. As you have seen and heard yesterday standing on the flowerpot at the window sill.

Scurrying up the concrete path she is wondering what she can say to me. I answer it trying to get it. I can't help her.

'Well, here's the *vehicle*, Ireen. Throw your case in the back. As you can see, the boys have left it in the hell of a mess.'

There are several pairs of scarred, muddy boots with knobbed soles, and these wads of newspapers with coloured drawings, stirred together, torn and trampled into the dust on the floor of Mrs Lockhart's car. The case thumps and bounces where you throw it, as she told you to. Glad to be rid of the hateful 'lunch'.

Now she is trying to start the car. It will not go.

'Asthmatic. But in the end it doesn't let you down.'

She is pressing and prodding and pulling at things. This is how she gets the wrinkles on her bottom. Wheezing and coughing out the smell of smoke. A bit asthmatic herself, it seems.

'There—you see—reliable!'

For the car has started to jerk and jump—to *go*. She is glad to show off its virtues.

But such an old rattling dirty car—is Mamma's sister poor perhaps? Then Mamma should see her as virtuous. But doesn't. More people hate than love one another.

If I had one of those lustrous, winged machines—Bentley, Lancia—would I have the courage to step on it and escape from the web of duties in which I am caught? Mornings like this demand winged cars and freedom, to match glistening water, gulls' wings, a ship breasting the swell at the Heads.

But I doubt my habits would be altered by a glamorous car.

Anyone observing me still following my beaten track in the winged Bentley delivering children to school, bullying greengrocers and butchers into letting me have their wartime produce cheap would interpret my behaviour as devotion to duty. Because I am outwardly an active, positive character ('bossy' to those who dislike me) not even enemies guess at my lack of will power and dread of being trodden on. Better say something to Ireen. 'Mr Harbord—the headmaster—is a man I can respect—and hope you will too.' She's probably not listening to you, foreigners are like that, they back away into their own language. 'Some parents—children too—find him too strict—but in such a *mixed* school—you'll see.'

Oh Lord children can make you feel idiotic. They know too much in some cases. Where the hell they get it from . . .

'I gather you haven't had much schooling.'

'There was Miss Adams when I was little.'

'Governesses were all very well in the past.'

'She didn't stay long. Mamma said they couldn't afford her.'

'I thought it was your father's aunt who paid.'

'Don't know.'

Trust Geraldine.

'Mamma says it depends on the parents—to civilise.'

'Civilisation—it's exams that count in real life. And anyway if your parents weren't there . . .'

'There was Aunt Cleone. She speaks five languages.'

'A very gifted old lady, I understand. Let's hope some of it has rubbed off on you Ireen. You'll need it.' I am talking the most utter cock, the sort of thing adults tell children—and one another, for that matter. 'One more bend, and I'll be able to show you your school.'

Poor kid's stiffening like a little cat.

'You know what I'm going to do. I'm going to stop a second and light up.' Grapple with the cellophane. Terrible how you can become dependent on a puff of smoke.

Ireen sits. I can feel gratitude for a reprieve seeping out of her. Stay here in this hot old car. It's what each of you would prefer. Don't think I ever grew up. On the other hand Ireen was born old. It could provide a meeting ground of sorts.

'That's better.' As the smoke tendrils grow upward against the windscreen like grey plants against the glass wall of a conservatory.

Say something. 'Out there amongst the rocks, that's lantana. It's a curse. I used to think it pretty, till I was told it wasn't. A great haunt for cats. Know it?'

'No-oh.'

It is neither pretty nor ugly—like so much so far. Mrs Lockhart is picking at a shred of tobacco stuck to her chapped, lower lip. Her teeth are stained and irregular. But this about the cats begins to make her Aunt Alison—Ally—I wish we could sit here forever amongst the invisible cats, disappear into the sun, the light, as it was in Greece before the war began. Mamma would not sit long enough, Ally might if you persuaded her.

As I can't talk to her in any language, she starts grunting, getting into gear, and we are driving round the last bend before the school. We are re-entering the streets of little purple and blood-red houses.

'There,' she says, 'see?' trying to make it sound exciting and important, though she is not the least bit excited. 'There's the school in the far block—set back a bit above the houses—*out of alignment*. D'you know what "alignment" is?'

'No.'

‘Well, it doesn’t matter. We think the old building has its architectural points. The rest is more or less temporary.’

The old building doesn’t look all that old, the whole school looks like a barracks at home, or sheds they have built for refugees, after a disaster. Aunt Cleone says we must be kind to all refugees, particularly those from Asia Minor.

She is pulling up in front of the school.

‘Bring your case, Ireen.’

She has two lines from her nostrils to the corners of her mouth. She sits a few moments behind the wheel after you have brought out the case with the lunch lurching round inside it. Then she takes out a lipstick from her bag and bloodies her mouth. She looks at herself in the little driver’s mirror, mumbling on her lips, working the stuff into the cracks. Aunt Cleone says only common women paint their mouths. I don’t think Mrs Lockhart—Aunt Ally—is common. Won’t she get out? We’ve got to go in.

It has become very hot inside the cold wind. The asphalt is blistering my feet as we cross it. Aunt Ally trips as her left foot loses contact with its platform. Cleonaki says the actors are wearing these high soles because that’s how it was in enacting the ancient tragedies.

As we approach, the building is humming with the voices of children at their lessons. Faces looking out here and there from windows are a fleshy grey like the leaves of plants grown behind glass.

Now we are clattering through this passage in the old building which has its architectural points. Aunt Ally seems to know without guidance how to find the headmaster's door. Her boys go to school here of course.

We are asked to come in.

Mr Harbord has been awaiting us. Wasn't I expected? He is a bald man with a stomach. He is wearing glasses which magnify his pale blue eyes. His smile magnifies his large teeth.

'How are we, Mrs Lockhart?' he asks, and laughs as though his question is a joke.

'Not bad, thank you, Mr Harbord.' Aunt Alison laughs, she has switched to another language, and sounds unlike what you came to think of as herself. 'This is my niece, Ireen Sklavos.' She stands smiling, working the lipstick into those cracks in her lips.

You are apparently the greater part of the joke Mr Harbord and Aunt Alison share.

Mr Harbord places a hand for a moment on the crown of your head, then removes it as though it has done its duty.

'How's Mr Lockhart?' Mr Harbord asks.

'The same,' Aunt Alison replies. 'I'm afraid it may be a duodenal ulcer.' Both look as grave as you have to.

We all sit down, behind and in front of the headmaster's desk, on which he places the broad tips of his white fingers. Against the smooth white flesh the wedding ring glistens more gold than gold.

'And Mrs Harbord?' Aunt Alison asks.

'Wellish,' he grumbles, and coughs, 'But still with her sister at Kiama.'

Aunt Alison begins scuffling her behind around in her chair, as preparatory to business.

'Ireen, I'm afraid,' she says, 'has had very little formal education.'

'No worry,' says Mr Harbord. 'Backward children often make the big jump forward.'

He smiles what is intended as the big, encouraging smile. 'What do you know, Reenie?'

Even as a joke it is too big a question. You can feel yourself blush like when Gilbert Horsfall asks you to explain the *pneuma*.

'I mean, what did they teach you over in Greece.'

'Miss Adams taught me to read and write—always in English. She taught me the names of the English kings. I learned French and German from my father's aunt. We read together Racine and Goethe. A little Shakespeare.'

'What you'd call a practical start in life.' Aunt Alison's teeth have grown brown and jagged again behind the cracks in her purple lips.

'What about Maths? Did they teach you your sums?' Mr Harbord persists.

'No-one was much good at mathematics. Mamma says she shed her materialistic Australian nature when she married with a Greek.'

I can feel my English growing worse as these people provoke me. Again I know my neck is blushing.

'Oho, I like *that*!' Aunt Alison cannot hold back a shriek. Mr Harbord's laughter sounds rubbery, sticky, like a tyre on a bumpy road.

When they compose themselves, Mr Harbord says, 'I hope we can put it back in you—some of the Australian character, I mean.'

He pushes back his chair and you all get up. You can tell this is the point at which something dreadful must happen.

We begin moving out of the headmaster's room, the lunch in Mrs Bulpit's case hardly thumping worse than your heart as Mr Harbord tells Aunt Alison '. . . start her at the beginning . . .' he nods for your benefit.

'I hope it won't be bad for you, Reenie, by giving you the opportunity to shine, we don't encourage that sort of thing.'

You want nothing more than to crawl away through the dark undergrowth of the garden over the warm moist leaf-mould, and perhaps re-join your fellow insects.

Where in all this zooming hive of horrible children is Gilbert Horsfall? Will he come in to defend you? Or will his acceptable blond nature be disgraced by association with the glistening black centipede admitted to this full classroom between the threatening bodies of Mr Harbord and Mrs Lockhart.

There is a tall thin additional threat in Miss Enderby standing in front of a blackboard on which a map has been drawn in coloured chalks. Mr Harbord, Mrs Lockhart, and Miss Enderby are all smiling too much for the child I no longer am.

Miss Enderby says, 'Move over, Viva. Make room for Ireen.'

Viva doesn't want to move, but does. She is dark, but not what you would call black, her white skin shows up what could be the beginnings of a moustache. She is frowning, perhaps afraid the others will blame her for having a foreigner next to her.

Miss Enderby has darted forward and takes hold of Mrs Bulpit's case, which you have begun to love, it is something you know. She stands the case as though it is in some way a thing of shame under the table on the platform. Bending down, or standing straight, Miss Enderby reminds you of a hairpin. Her skin is a pale, shabby brown. Though her face is fairly young, it is raked with lines, her hair of no particular colour looks dusty from the grey in it. Blue eyes might look pretty if she wasn't so worried.

Mr Harbord's large teeth are on display. 'Easy does it, Miss Enderby. We've got to get to know one another. Then it'll be fine.'

'That's correct, Mr Harbord.' Miss Enderby's smaller teeth snicker back uneasily at her superior, and she rearranges the unused hankie stuck through a bangle on her thin brown forearm.

Standing to attention in front of the blackboard on which she has drawn the map of Australia festooned with signs of various kinds, the teacher could have been caught out at something. Mrs Lockhart, too, looks caught, and is glad to fade away with her embarrassment, piloted by the headmaster after flicking his head at Ireen Sklavos. It is meant to encourage you.

Classmates jab their elbows into the ribs of two boys at the back. From the look of them they could be middle Lockharts embarrassed by their mother's showing up at school. Avoid these Lockharts.

Will Gilbert Horsfall's voice never break through the partition separating you from other cells in this thundering hive?

Miss Enderby stands a moment, head bowed, above her table, collecting her scattered thoughts, then flicks back her dusty hair, the not quite pretty blue eyes stare or glare at the distance.

'As Captain Cook sailed up what we know today as the coast of Queensland, he sighted a group of mountains singular in shape. He called them . . .' as the eyes withdraw from the distance of history they focus on a present target '. . . What did he call them—Viva Jenkins? Tell us, please, in case Ireen Sklavos hasn't heard.'

Viva Jenkins looks livid. You can feel yourself turning green on being singled out in front of all these children. Viva will blame you for this moment forever.

'The Glasshouse Mountains,' Viva Jenkins answers coldly quickly through thinned lips.

Miss Enderby's glass stare looks appeased. She sails on up the coast to wherever the blue arrows will take her, past Aegean rocks in a tropical sea. Yellow tracks leading into the interior widen into human footprints. The sun hangs heavier than August on Aiyina. The classroom is rocking by now with the swell of the sea. Hidden in the mangroves blacks are waiting to spear the landing parties of explorers. [Find out about these mangroves].

You look at Viva, this black moustache against the white skin. It is you who are the black. Her lips, her eyelashes, her fringe all hate you. She takes this pin and sticks it into your foreign arm. You both sit staring at the pinprick of blood which swells which overflows. Black speared by white amongst the treacherous mangroves.

You cannot prevent your eyes overflowing. Viva is a glassy blur. The black mangrove fringe. Something of Viva herself is ebbing away with your blood. Her white forehead is swelling. Her thin lips begin to glow as though from the wound she has opened in your flesh.

Miss Enderby's lesson is foundering somewhere in the islands to the north. Nobody here, Miss Enderby included, knows about islands.

She arranges her chalks, her pencils, and a squelchy yellow rubber on the table. A chalk-saturated duster makes her cough.

Since the lesson is over everyone comes spilling out from behind the desks, bumping, slamming, feet grating. Screams and babbles break from mouths as they jostle anybody in their way. The two freckly Lockharts jump and kick sideways like frisky horses.

There is no question of their knowing a cousin even though they may know about her. All to the good.

Miss Enderby remembers, and picks up the offending case from beneath her table. 'Viva, look after Ireen—show her the ropes—where to leave her case. Cases, Ireen, are not brought into class.'

She has done her duty. In the purple brown mash of her face, perspiring white circles of skin make the eyes look more remote than ever.

Viva, it seems, is more the outcast than Ireen as all the children tear past.

'Take your case,' Viva mumps through a heavy disgust as thick as phlegm. 'This is when we eat lunch.'

'Already?'

'Yair. You arrived late, didn't you?'

In the circumstances Viva even seems to think that what should be a virtue amounts to a sin.

Under the fronds of this tree with its little pink berries you look at each other munching lunches. Viva may have forgotten the blood that flowed in class. Munching helps. Mrs Bulpit has provided something pale that tastes of sawdust between slices of soggy bread. There is a wizened apple. Viva has much the same. Her teeth bulge with doughy bread. She rejects crusts.

'Wossat?'

'Chocolate.'

'Got chocolate for school lunch?'

You can't care.

Viva is soon chocolate-lipped. 'You see these two girls coming over? They're reffoes. They'll try anything on. Got all the cheek in the world.'

The girls are sort of smiling. Their blenched nostrils are scenting chocolate. One girl's ears are pierced for little golden rings. But the second girl's lobes have real earrings suspended from them, little coral stones trembling like the berries of the shade tree under which we have been eating our lunch. This girl wears an actual ring on her plump finger, with a stone in it.

She grins and says, 'You're eating chocolate. My uncle manufactures . . .'

'Okay, Lily,' Viva warns, clamping her teeth on a last piece, 'we know about your uncle's chocolate.'

'Ireen can't if she is *new*.'

'I do, don't I? And Reenie's my friend.'

The two girls do not seem discouraged. You wish you were as tough. Not even Viva is as tough as Lily and her friend, or perhaps it is her sister.

The girl with the little gold rings in her ears becomes very confidential as she asks, 'Are you one of us, Ireen—are you?'

‘How?’ It is once more exhausting, even frightening.

The two girls look at you so closely, it is like some Greeks trying to find out whether you are red or black, Mamma always says when it comes to politics it is best to keep your mouth shut.

‘Piss off, Eva—Lily, she’s not,’ Viva hisses through a spray of chocolate.

Eva and Lily are not put out. As they walk away they are wreathed in disbelieving smiles and pity for one who is Viva Jenkins’ friend.

‘Bloody reffoes!’ Viva grumbles.

She starts to wipe her mouth with her hand but thinks better and takes out a tissue which she drops afterwards on the asphalt which tree roots have lifted up.

‘If you want the toilet, Reenie, the GIRLS is down there, but the boys can give trouble.’

‘Thank you. I think I will hold out.’

Not long after the bell rings.

‘This is Maths. You don’t have to worry. It isn’t any trouble. Nobody bothers about Mr Manley. He’s a poof, but Elsie Chapman has a crush on him for something to do.’

As we go up towards the classroom, Viva turns, as though no blood has flowed between us. ‘I’m glad you’re my friend, Ireen.’ She is heavy as ever. Perhaps she has no other friends. Mr Manley is short, plump, a puffy white. His thick-lensed spectacles might be helping him not to see the faces he is addressing. His hands fly about like big velvety butterflies battering themselves against the blackboard on which he is demonstrating weights and measures. Boys laugh and aim paper darts, one of them hits the blackboard just missing Mr Manley's hand as he scribbles elegant figures in chalk. He does not seem to notice. The girls hold conversations, share secrets. Only Elsie Chapman attends. She is sitting chin-on-hand watching Mr Manley's display. No sign of Lily and Eva, they are surely cleverer and in a higher class.

All these weights and measures bring back the scales in Aunt Cleonaki's kitchen with Evthymia weighing out flour for *koulourakia*. Her peasant hands are as rough red and stiff as Mr Manley's palpitating butterflies are white and delicate. There is the same sadness in flour and chalkdust rising through the murmur of an afternoon. Will it never be over?

'When you come to my place,' Viva whispers, 'I'll show you something my father brought with him from Patagonia. He got it in Brazil.'

Oh, no! Brazil, Patagonia yes, but never Viva's place. The only escape is through Gilbert Horsfall who will probably never come.

• • •

It is over. The homework is set. How will you, who are homeless, do any homework and what? You have wet yourself a little, will they see, down the left leg.

Elsie Chapman lays a flower, or part of one, on Mr Manley's desk. He is afraid she does not mean it. His soft damp parti-moustache is flopping up and down as he laughs his disbelief.

'They're a couple of silly sooks. She does it at every lesson. She snitches them over the fences on her way to school. Doesn't mean it, of course—not with Lionel Manley. Showed her pussy to Gil Horsfall in break.'

So it is over. Someone has slammed the lid of a desk.

'I have to get back to where I am living. They—my aunt, Mrs Lockhart—didn't tell me what to do.'

'You're in Cameron Street, aren't you? Mumma and Essie Bulpit are mates. Lockharts live in the opposite direction. Don't worry we'll take the bus, I'll show you where to get off, Reenie.'

It is too awful, and at the bus stop with our cases. How does Gilbert Horsfall get back?

'Where does Elsie Chapman live?'

'Balmoral way,' Viva waves. 'Her father mostly fetches her in the vehicle. They're an influential family.

He has a refrigeration business. Gee,' she says, 'Reenie, I'm so glad to have you for my friend.'

If only the Australian asphalt would receive your melting flesh, amongst the squashed fruit from this great hairy tree.

'I have no money for any bus.'

'Don't worry. I'll give you the lend of the fare.'

There is no escaping. We are so close, our cases clash and almost tangle together in skeins of twisting soft chocolate. There is a dog's shit lying on the kerb.

Boys' heavy shoes are cracking the pavement open. Their voices cackle, something about '. . . stone the tarts . . .'

'Don't worry, they'll cool down,' Viva hisses, she turns her back.

Two older, spotty boys, tufts of hair amongst the skin and—Gilbert Horsfall. Gilbert doesn't see—he has never seen you. He cackles worse than his spotted friends, grinds his shoes into the pavement and bashes the treetrunk with his case. Will Aunt Ally at the last moment rescue you from the heavy web in which you are netted—of Viva Jenkins, the tufted boys, and Gilbert Horsfall.

Nothing happens for the best. The boys shove past the girls and sit at the back of the bus. Viva pushes you into a seat near the driver.

'How's my little lady?' the driver asks.

'Good, thanks. This is my friend Ireen. She's a Greek just arrived from Greece.'

'Waddaya know!' The driver can't help but look sideways from dragging on the wheel, steering the bus round a difficult corner.

The boys at the back crow and fall about. Some of the corners are close shaves, though never as close as in Greece.

You feel you may be sick, not from the bus, but from everything, including Viva's serge tunic.

She is so helpful. 'This is it, Reenie—the stop for Cameron. Keep straight on down. I'll keep a look out in the morning.'

Her chocolate hands are unwilling to let you go. What if she succeeds in keeping you there and you have to face her Mumma?

But another body is pushing past. It is hard and wiry, the shoe hurts that kicks you just above the heel.

Gilbert Horsfall's face is ugly as he waves back at his two friends. Ought to wave back at Viva, but you can't. Ought to feel grateful.

When the bus has disappeared, Gilbert turns. 'How're you making out, Irene?' He is talking the language you understand, his face is the one you recognise as Gilbert Horsfall's.

'I don't know.' Mustn't cry.

You walk a bit together. He makes no attempt to draw away. A wrist slithers against yours, which makes it worse—and beautiful.

'I hate it!' You could have been sticking a pin into Viva Jenkins' slab of an arm.

'Yes,' he agrees, but only vaguely. 'Feel better when you get a load of Ma Bulpit's bread and dripping inside you.'

She was out when you arrived. 'Scoop it out for ourselves, specially the brown bit underneath. It's delicious.'

'Mrs Bulpit's name is Essie. Viva told me.'

'Mm?'

You go out together into the garden, which at this hour seems to be hanging above the water, floating without support from the precipice.

Essie Bulpit has turned out the 'lovely room' she has for you.

'Don't know how I got through it—considering . . .'

She breaks wind as she opens the door and leads the way.

'. . . considering the state of my health . . . might have taken on more than I can cope with . . .'

The 'lovely room' is still more or less a box room.

'Of course you'll appreciate, Ireen, I've got to keep my own belongings *somewhere*—in me own home.'

Essie Bulpit's pastry figure, and against the opposite wall the black dressmaker's dummy make a pair of caryatids guarding these sacred objects.

She burps again, 'Ah, dear' and swallows 'Mrs Haggerty down the road's got it—well, I'm not going to dwell on it. Can't allow black thoughts, can we? Won't help the *war effort*.' She laughs, and her teeth clack together.

At the far end of the room Essie has arranged a narrow bed, or ottoman. There is also a small chest, a table and chair.

'. . . do your homework—write home to your mum . . .'

More important are the two windows through which the light from the water floats upward through the branches of the dark trees.

Till thankfulness is invaded by the tanks and armoured cars of fear. 'Where is Gilbert?'

'Expect he's started on his homework. And you ought to get busy with yours.'

'Don't know what it is.'

She sighs in going out. 'Ah dear—don't expect it matters—all that much.'

Since this morning Mrs Bulpit's eyes don't seem to have the world in their sights.

This room she has got ready for you has started to become yours, not from any effort on your part, but simply by your being there. This could be something to remember, to use as a consolation for being anywhere at all. Whether in this floating half-light or later when you have undressed (a nightie makes you feel sadder) and got into bed. Bed is no more than this narrow padded box disguised as one. The brown wartime electricity will not be more comfort than darkness. Dreams must grow out of either. A black caryatid on the march is stuck with pins from which sawdust flows instead of blood. Miss Enderby expecting homework from the homeless. Mr Manley does not expect anyway not Elsie's flower ringed with fur. You dare go down because you must to the GIRLS where there are no girls only boys Gil is tearing off your clothes he is wearing his ugly school face his voice his laughter that of the others surrounding us. They are laughing at this baby's wrinkle to which you have shrunk from what was once a mouth down between the brown spots through the hole where you parted with Mamma long before the ship sailed down to the source of shame welling out first as a warm trickle then as the deafening cold roar of the cistern inside the wooden shed.

All quiet inside your deafened room not yet dawn perhaps if you lie long enough this warm wet will disappear nothing ever does at Thebes they are drying up the swamp to wipe out malaria deserve to catch it such a big girl from lying in your own dirty swamp Essie's pointing finger has this transparent thimble on it which needles have pricked.

The blue light of dawn starts to flow in through the crack in the curtain clean water shadows lapping over this stagnant swamp where you are lying. The black dummy and the furniture are ticking away in league with all that is stagnant and malarial.

Gil will know. If you can reach him.

Bulpit snores are sighing sucking ebbing and returning.

Gil has drawn the curtains. It is carved GIL on his naked statue lying in these pools of milky light quarried brought just recently from Paros. Disturb a dream it will dissolve into disgust or hate. Cannot risk. But grope back, your own damp black rags of misery trailing behind.

If you could only die but you don't only old people or soldiers in a war or Papa murdered they say.

So it is morning. And the wet is drier. But not enough. Will become a stain of shame in any case.

In time you learn to do your homework. You learn to learn, or forget what you have learnt from Miss Adams Great Aunt Cleone Evthymia Mamma Papa the Greek earth.

The Australian Democracy is not interested in politics when there's a war to be fought and won a Japanese menace submarines did you ever in Sydney Harbour but the Yanks are here the Americans will save us.

Life is rumours and newspapers. Viva Jenkins says Elsie Chapman laid down with a GI in the scrub above Balmoral and he give her a packet of cigarettes. She said it was immense.

Mrs Bulpit says, 'You don't know what to make of young people nowadays.' Perhaps it is because she is missing out on experience that has made her shrink. She no longer looks made of freshly steamed suet crust. She is baked yellow, a short crust with dust in the cracks. 'Don't know what Gil and you get up to. How you get your homework done in no time. What the teachers think of it. It isn't natural. Mucking around out there in the garden.'

Gil mumbles, 'We're building a house.'

'A house? Well, I never.'

'A cubby.'

'A cubby indeed. One minute you're grown up, the next you're kids again.'

It is not altogether like this because you have always been grown up if they only knew. Mrs Bulpit will never understand that what he tells her is a cubby or a house is neither—or is and isn't.

It started not long after the first day (and night) at school. You learn what is expected after a fashion. Homework for instance. You learn to use your voice, a different language. You learn that Miss Enderby lives with her sister, that Mr Manley is expected to have a nervous breakdown, you learn all about diseases, and the bloods (never really learn about the bloods, will Mrs Bulpit find them on what she calls the *ottoman*?). It started on an evening when a dead bat (they call them flying foxes here) fell out of the big tree on the cliff edge where GILBERT HORSFALL has carved his name. The air is very still, neither warm nor cold, in what they still call winter, when Gil shouts in the raw school voice you have never liked, 'Come on, for Chrissake, we gotter do something.' And drives the knife into the bark where words end.

He roams around fossicking, nearly stumbles on what he kicks ('all this *Wandering Jew* stuff') and brings out these old still hard boards which the weeds and time have not succeeded in rotting.

'Why don't we build something, Eirene,' remembering Mamma perhaps, because no-one else in Australia has called you Eirene, not till now, and will probably never. 'Why don't we put a platform in the tree—where we can climb up to—and sit.'

He is breathing hard as he frees the boards, rank juices making us sneeze, his long whole bony face thinking.

Would it be wrong to love Gilbert Horsfall's face? To love somebody. He will kill you if he knows.

Help him drag the boards. Drag them up the tree. Arms of a silky sinewy white monkey. Gilbert Horsfall is doing it all. A hard hand helps drag me up, like some old board. Only when he has arranged the boards, says he must get a hammer and nails, and we are crouching there on our platform, you will know what to tell, say, do. Stroke your throat waiting for this moment you might have dreamt about now forming in the fork of this black tree.

But the blood, will it trickle down on the platform, and farther, through the cracks in our house?

Viva says, 'Elsie Chapman's wearing the rags. That'll curb the cow. It's nothing, though, Lily and Eva have to take a bath. Essie Bulpit—*everybody* knows. It's only the boys don't understand. Boys are stoopid. Didn't your auntie Mrs Lockhart tell you about it?'

'If ever there's anything you want to ask me, ask, Ireen.' Never see Aunt Ally, or almost never, now.

It turns out that Mrs Bulpit knows '. . . something that happens to all of us . . .' from finding it on this *ottoman* called a bed. '. . . not to worry, Ireen. Ah, dear . . .'

She would rather not be faced with things, even those she knows about.

Gilbert Horsfall is the one who must have either the grinning mask of the ivory monkey he puts on with other boys, or stretched out lying on the floor of our house, elbows pointing at a moon which has not yet come alive, a silver disk before it starts to palpitate with the unborn twins behind its thin skin. Or *pneuma* you will never talk about again with G. HORSFALL or anybody.

He says, 'This is nothing like. We've got to do something about it—make it real.'

He says 'we' but means 'he'. You are just there as a kind of shadow to his ideas.

He gets hold of a load of old hessian through somebody, think it's the brother-in-law of Mr Burt the bus driver everybody likes. We—or Gil makes walls for the house out of musty hessian. The hair is sprouting in his armpits. Moisture trembles down from the tips of the pinkish hairs.

Gil says, 'That's okay. But not the real thing, d'you think?' as though expecting you to give an answer.

He thought of the biscuit tin, the upright Arnott's Arrowroot one, washed out. He borrows the brace-and-bit from the bus driver's brother-in-law. And tin cutters so that he can tear a hole in the bottom of the biscuit tin. He tears his hand. He bores the hole in the platform, or floor of our house, bleeding and sweating all the time.

'There,' he says, 'we've got a dunny now,' and wants me to sit on the biscuit tin and let him hear I am peeing in our dunny.

Once Mrs Bulpit passes underneath and calls up, 'You kids up there, what are you doing I'd like to know?' Her head tilted back, and her mouth, her plastic teeth open, like as if she is laughing when she isn't.

'House-keeping' Gil answers back, kind of not laughing too.

She closes her mouth. 'I wouldn't expect to be cheeked by better class children.'

'But it isn't cheek—it's *true*!' Has his voice begun to break, or is it just the schoolboy's cockerel laughter?

You are sitting on the Arnott's dunny where to please Gil you have learnt to pee. Now you have begun, you can't stop on any account.

'And this—raining down. I hope it's nothing rude—I can't stand rudery—not in my state of health.'

'It's nothing, Mrs Bulpit. Only a possum.' You jam your thighs together.

'A possum by daylight? Not likely.'

He pulls you down beside him on the platform, and you lie side by side like the snipers in the mountains in the presence of the enemy.

'I don't believe anything anyone tells me, not since I last saw Doctor.'

Through the knothole you can see her trying to trace a deceit. She closes her teeth. She clears her throat, and walks away. Staggering slightly, to her *real* house.

He puts his hand where the pee is still wet, that he has called up, then pulls his same hand away, it could have been scalded.

I would like to tell him something. I would like to write, or better, speak, the poem G. has put into me. I I I show Gilbert Horsfall that I am me me me. Not a mewing cat. He might stroke me if I were, which I would not want, or do I?

I shall not write this poem. Memory is safer than invisible ink, that all the school knows about, playing at spies, exchanging coded messages.

Lily Feizenbaum comes up in break, looking more than usually mysterious. She shoves a folded paper in the pocket of your cardy. Unfolded, the paper is perfectly blank.

'What has she given you?' Viva is always on the watch.

'A sheet of paper.'

'Betcher that's the old invisible ink. You hold it up to heat and it brings the writing out. See? Silly nonsense. I wouldn't want to know what Feizenbaums have to write you. So you needn't tell me.'

Your pocket could hardly wait. You heat the stove. Essie was out, Gilbert mucking around outside, on one of the days when he gets sick of you. You hold Lily's blank paper to the flame (what if you burned it and never got to know?).

The message grew, a yellow brown spidery.

Momma says you are welcome any Shabbat night at our table. Lily F.

'Hi there,' Gil's voice, 'where've you got to.'

Hold the paper quickly to the flame.

'What's that?'

The paper melted into tinkling ash. 'Some notes I don't need any more.'

'Not cribbing?'

Better not to answer.

'Come on out and do something!'

Climb up behind him, into our tree, our house. He falls down grinding his neck into the heap of old hessian snippets we use as pillows. 'Christ, it's *boring*! We gotter think of something to do . . .'

I stand looking out through the doorway of the house above the hanging garden. We will always mean *I*. He does not want me. What if I speak the invisible poem I feel inside me. Will it give me back the power I thought I had on coming here? The poem that cannot be put into words.

• • •

Inside these musty, suffocating walls, this lumpy heap of pricking hessian. Bruce Lockhart knew a bloke who caught the crabs. They shaved him around the cock, armpits too, and painted him blue. Anything could crawl out of a heap of filthy old hessian.

What would they say if they saw you painted blue in the dunny at school?

'I'm gunner walk around a bit.'

Shake her off. This girl got in his hair at times.

He swung down quickly out of the tree to show he did not need her company. He would have walked over to Lockharts', only the old man might stare him out. 'He mightn't even know your name. Who are you?' 'I'm Gilbert Horsfall—sir,' 'Who?' Hang around outside while they had their tea. Till the boys came out. They still mightn't want him. He hunched his shoulders trying to count up the people who might know about and want him. The Colonel knew, but you couldn't say he *wanted*. After that Ma Bulpit, Irene Sklavos, the teachers while you were in class, the Ballards if they hadn't forgotten. His list petered out.

Walking down the winding, swooping streets he said his name 'GILBERT HORSFALL!' He liked it, but turned round, in case somebody might have heard and thought him a nut. He liked to run his hands over his body. Nobody ever noticed it. It was there, though.

The evening swirled around him. Lights were coming on in some of the homes. An old woman was cuddling a cat on a veranda. Old people. Running her fingers through the cat fur. She had lifted it up and was rubbing noses with the bloody cat. They say a cat has worms in its nose. This old dried up woman had it coming to her if she didn't know enough by the time she had reached well, fifty at least. Old people got on his tits.

From time to time he pinched his nipples, they itched rather pleasantly, then harder till it hurt.

He didn't like to think about the old nipples of the woman playing with her cat. The girl on the beach had covered them up as soon as she saw you were looking at what was red and rubbery, sort of flowers cut out of a wet bathing cap.

Sandy skin. What if you sucked on a tit that had been making flowerpots in the sand . . .

Bruce knew a bloke who got the clap or siph or whatever it was from going with a woman down at Mrs Macquarie's Seat.

Must be somebody who hasn't got it.

In the street he was walking down lined with big fuchsias, tree fuchsias, it was already oily dark. The deep blue sky had begun prickling slightly with stars. In a lit window a man was grinding his mouth in a woman's open one backwards and forwards like he was swallowing her down, all the while running his hands. Some of them had brown nipples (Bruce says they don't have to be boongs).

Gilbert bloody Horsfall tore off a branch of the giant fuchsia and whipped the darkness. Tassels flew in all directions. The soft, fleshy, sticky stems.

He threw the mangled remains away.

Ohhhh he groaned, swallowing the warm damp sea air, gulping at the stars, he would have swallowed them down if he had been close enough. What was the point of anything at all? Run away, and join up and get killed. A hero on a memorial. Eirene Sklavos had seen killing, if you could believe her. Her father had been murdered. All bullsh probably. But what she had seen, done and knew stuck like splinters in his mind.

Less murders nowadays. Ma Bulpit said it was because there's a war on. Not without a soldier murders some girl for holding out on him. There was the boy the sailor murdered. Pervs. There was that sailor at Neutral Bay who let down his apron and waved his dick at you. Like you were a perv. You weren't—or were you?

He lurched round the bend, reeling, like on a ship in a rolling sea beneath the high swirling wastes of an ultra-marine, prickling sky, fell down at last on a bit of wasteland above a culvert, lashing out at lantana and the wiry trailers of morning glory as the stones ate into his back? Or were there others around him in the darkness?

Big boongs with coffee coloured nipples, blousy girls with cut outs of red bathing-cap rubber. Experienced guys in business suits and moustaches grinding into unwilling mouths. Sailor on sailor.

He was so hard he got to pulling it off, moaning for the stones, lantana smelling of cat piss and semen, the cold blue enamel of the sky. And lay wilting, not crying, it was sweat—or semen.

He had shrunk right into himself into a kind of guilty purity he had never experienced that he could remember. Wondering what Irene Sklavos would have thought. Why, for Chrissake, this Ireen, who was nothing to do with him. But might have been standing over him looking down, prissy lips pressed together, like she had just been not explaining the bleeding *pneuma*. Haunting him on this wasteland above the culvert.

He sat up presently, buttoned his fly, and started the walk towards Cameron Street. He felt drained. His legs could have been parcels of straw. As he brushed against the hedge of giant fuchsias, he was sprinkled with drops so cold and silver he shuddered for his own enormity. Were they eyes glittering amongst the foliage and fleshy tassels? What odds? She was nothing to him, another kid, a *girl*, a Greek reffo Lockharts said was her mother's bastard.

When he got in there was no sound from the other side of her door. Must have gone to bed. He could see her lying on that ottoman like a queen on a tomb. He could hear the sounds of furniture and dry rot inside Ma Bulpit's dunny.

His own room, under the warrant officer's leaning portrait, was one big yawn tonight. Neither light nor darkness let him alone. He lay remembering forever all that he most wanted to forget. And Eirene Sklavos was advancing on him her plait trailing across the carpet behind her like a long black snake, its tail still had to enter the room when she had almost reached his bedside.

'. . . running late . . . miss the bus if you're not careful . . .' It was Ma Bulpit's voice twitching him awake.

To do him an extra favour she poured out his tea for him this morning. Her pink chenille had some egg in it.

Sklavos had had her breakfast. Her plate with the slops of crispies in it is standing on the table opposite.

'Where's Irene?'

'Finishing something for school.' The Bulpit had not yet put in her teeth, didn't bother at that hour and for kids, her hair still had a sleepy look, she might have been rootling round in her head for something to start complaining about.

Finished his breakfast as quick as he could.

Ireen—she looked like Eirene this morning—was sitting at that table at the end of her room where the stored furniture thinned out and the empty space became hers. A clear light fell around her from the window. The ottoman-bed was already made. When she looked up she might have been suggesting he should have knocked, giving him the cold look of a grown-up woman.

'What are you doing?' he heard himself bleating as he advanced.

'Work,' she answered, colder than ever, and lowered her eyes.

'You must have gone to bed early,' he tried it out cautiously.

Had she smelled him out? The dry scales of it were rustling between his thighs.

'What's this?'

She sat colouring in the drawing of a spray of flowers. Beside the paper lay a fuchsia branch, the sap still fresh where torn off, the leaves only just beginning to wilt, tassels drooping.

'We were set an essay on our favourite flower.' The purple and cerise glowed deeper as she worked.

'But a fuchsia can't be your favourite flower! Nobody would ever think about the fuchsia . . .'

'There are roses of course. You've never seen a Greek rose.'

He hadn't but her voice conveyed proud blooms of a noble size.

'You can like something all of a sudden,' she said, returning to the flower she was giving life, 'something you've never thought about before. Then you might forget about it.'

She got up briskly after that, gathered her drawing and the pages of her essay, and laid them in her case.

'We don't want to miss the bus.'

Her eyes seemed to have elongated, their whites glittered at him for an instant, as the light had through the branches of the fuchsia hedge.

'Yair,' he said, 'the bus.'

And followed her plait out of the room.

• • •

That night, after they had shed the bus people, he couldn't wait to ask, 'How did you go with your essay and the drawing?'

'They didn't seem to think much of them.'

Viva said, 'I'm gunner get off at your stop, Reenie, because Mumma has a message for Mrs Bulpit, who she hasn't seen for a long while.'

You could not do anything about it. If you cut off one of Viva's tentacles, she grew another. She was the Australian octopus.

She said, 'Remember that droring of the fuchsia—I thought it was beaut, Ireen. My old dahlia—I can't say I don't like a dahlia but . . . fuchsias are different. Nobody would ever think of a fuchsia—the way they hang . . .'

Viva did not have a limp, her shoe only caught rather often in the cracked pavement as she slommacked along.

Mrs Bulpit wasn't home. Gil must have escaped quickly from the bus mob, put together his bread and dripping, and vanished. The aluminium dripping bowl still looked to be rocking on the kitchen table.

Viva eyed the bowl while combating her saliva. 'Isn't this a spooky house?'

'I haven't noticed.' Viva's presence made you defend what had become once more your property, it was more yours than Mrs Bulpit's and this afternoon, even Gil Horsfall's.

'Where's that nasty bugger of a Horsfall boy?'

'I don't know.' You could truthfully say.

'I don't like him,' Viva persisted.

'You don't know him—only at school.'

'I know enough. Ooh, I don't like this house! He might jump out and interfere with us.'

'He's never tried to interfere with *me*.'

'Must be a perv then—like they say—and I've always thought.'

'He's my friend.'

'Wouldn't want a perv for a friend—or any nasty boy.'

Their conversation was leading them out of the kitchen and down those ricketty steps which led to the back yard and garden. The steps threatened to pitch Viva into it too quickly.

The need to protect Gil increased Eirene's feeling of power.

'You didn't show me your room,' Viva complained as she landed in the yard flat on her feet.

'No, I didn't.' It's only a sort of box room. You could not bear the thought of Viva staring at the hard narrow ottoman-bed and fossicking amongst dusty objects which from time to time had furnished your dreams.

What she had been spared inspired Eirene to leap, missing out the short flight of ricketty rotting wooden steps. Her sense of power and release made her feel she was flying. She landed lightly at Viva Jenkins' heels, and at once let out a cry filled with disgust, pain and giggles.

'What's up, Ireen?' Viva had turned, frowning under her dark fringe.

'I squashed a—long—black—*slug*!'

As proof the slug lay mashed and quivering on its deathbed of disintegrating concrete, while Eirene sounded as though she might die of all that was churning out of her.

'Only a slug! You're the real loop, Ireen.'

If they had not drifted deeper into the garden and come across something of greater interest, Viva Jenkins might have reconsidered her friendship with this loopy Greek reffo.

'What's that up there?'

'That's a house—a cubby.'

'Who built it?'

'We did—Gil and I.'

'And you go up there together?'

'We used to—sometimes . . .'

Eirene Sklavos feels the power fainting inside her.

'Can we go up?'

'It isn't safe. The boards are rotten.' Fainter and fainter Eirene Sklavos hears herself. 'Mrs Bulpit forbids it.' The school language she has learnt to speak is ebbing out of her.

Worst of all, Gil could be up there listening.

As Viva suspects, 'Could be up there all the while.'

The evening is drawing in. Bats have begun flying.

'Ooh, it's grooby! Land in yer hair. Can't stay all night waiting for old Essie to show up.'

The light has intensified her fringe and her mole.

'When you come to my place, Reenie, I'll show you what my father brought from Brazil,' she stands threatening an instant at the gate.

Viva was standing at the gate, waiting. 'Thought you wasn't coming.' She might have preferred it that way. 'Mumma said you wouldn't. Said from what she'd heard you'd be too grand.'

The kind of remark you had learnt to ignore.

Jenkins' place was an 'old' house. The gate might have fallen down if Viva hadn't been persuading it to stand. The weatherboard house had once been painted, but by now the paint had almost flaked away. It had the look of some old Arab house outside Alexandria which had soaked up a lifetime of sunlight, and this absorption was perhaps what helped it hold together. A one-eyed house, with a lace curtain veiling that. There were several additional windows, but all of them bare, which gave them a blind glassy look. A pretty fretwork balcony above the porch had a couple of floorboards hanging from it.

'I like your balcony,' you told her for something to say. 'I'd spend half my time up there, looking out across the water.'

'It isn't safe,' she warned as though getting her own back.

She was leading you up the front steps. The wooden uprights were each decorated with a pyramid, the point of the one you put your hand on so metal-sharp it made you squeal.

'Ooooh! That's dangerous!'

'That's what my father said when he fell off the balcony and landed on it.'

'He could have been killed. Was he badly hurt?'

'We don't know. He disappeared.'

Viva's mum had been waiting for them somewhere in the dark interior behind the lace. When she showed up, she was wearing an easy cotton dress in no particular style. Standing side by side with her daughter, she was not much taller.

'Hello Ireen,' Mrs Jenkins said, 'I'm glad to meet Viva's friend at last.' She had a smile which came and went, like thin sunlight, and several teeth were missing in one side of a pink denture. The dark room made her skin look whiter. She was one of those women who had been steamed rather than baked by the Sydney climate.

She said, 'I expect you'll have a lot to tell me,' and planted herself on the edge of a sofa.

Did she really expect? It could have been expectation which caused her white calves to bulge when she wrapped her arms around her knees. Her feet were bare except for a pink corn plaster.

Viva was scowling with embarrassment. 'Aren't you gunner give 'er something to eat?'

'You're just like your father! Think of nothing but feeding your face. Nice people when they come to see you expect a bit of intercourse. Viva,' she confided in Irene, 'can never hope to become a lady.'

Viva could have been suppressing a whimper somewhere inside her muttering.

'Do they live in houses like this in Greece?' Mrs Jenkins asked her visitor. 'Are they Christians?'

'I suppose so.'

'Mr Jenkins was a pagan.'

'He was *not*!'

'You can't expect anything of most men.' Mrs Jenkins was becoming vehement. A wind swept through her listless hair. 'There's the gas—he promised me to come last Thursday and it's now this Tuesday. We could die of it for all he cares.' She opened her small white ringless hands and glanced not so much at the hands as a nothingness she was holding in them.

There was certainly a smell of gas in the room. It became the stronger for your noticing it. The coloured plastic flowers seemed to exude the smell of gas.

Mrs Jenkins must have noticed you noticing. 'I love plastic flowers, don't you? I think they're more artistic than the real, which die on a person anyway.'

The gaseous colours of the plastics glowed.

Suddenly Mrs Jenkins jumped up so quickly she had to steady herself on the end of the sofa. 'Suppose I'd better bring you something to eat or this girl of mine will go crook on me. You'll have to entertain Maureen, dear, while I'm out of the room.'

'She's mad,' Viva said, 'Mr Horan—that's the gas

feller—came on Thursday, but she wouldn't let him alone. He left without finishing the job.'

'Why don't we open the window—let the gas escape?'

Viva became more agitated. 'Wouldn't be worth it. She doesn't want anything to escape. That's why Carlos disappeared.'

'Carlos?'

'My father—Charlie to his mates—but Carlos was his name. I'll tell you all about that. No pagan,' she glanced at the doorway through which her mother had just gone 'my father was a mystic.'

Irene Sklavos felt her eyelids snap as though she were awakening to a state she had sensed but never been able to put a name to. From Aunt Cleonaki she had learnt about the Saints, all of them far too Orthodox and rigid for the word to apply. She suspected Cleonaki would have disapproved of anything so fluid. If you knew about mystics yourself it was from associating with the state in certain dreams and an imagination you had to keep hidden.

She could feel her heart palpitating like a rubber bulb. 'You must tell me about your father, Viva, because I think I understand—sort of,' she added to appease the part of herself which had learnt to be Australian.

Viva brushed back her fringe. 'I'll tell you and show you—when she's out of the way. But you must promise never to tell. It will always be our secret.'

In speaking of her father Viva's speech seemed to improve, her voice vibrated like some stringed instrument—a 'cello?

Irene saw that Viva might be acquiring power over her, but could not resist promising. A moment of complete physical repugnance occurred as she visualised herself sharing a warm bath with Viva Jenkins. As the water lapped against the sides of the bath it revealed a greasy highwater mark.

'Ssh!' Viva warned. 'She's coming.'

Mrs Jenkins had restored her face with smiles and a forced tranquillity. She was carrying a dish, on it a clutch of little cakes, and a jug of what looked like lemonade, but as remote from the lemon as her plastic flowers were from soil, sunlight, and natural grace. The jug of pseudo lemonade shared their gaseous glow.

'These are very special cakes,' Mrs Jenkins smiled, 'from a recipe of my grandmother's.'

'Ah, them.' Viva sounded disenchanted.

A rancid taste was soon mingling in Irene with the smell of gas.

Viva refused a cake, but began slurping at a glassful of the green lemonade.

Had Mrs Jenkins perhaps set out to poison you, and did Viva, the false friend, know of her mother's intention? Together they would bury the body in the gas-saturated soil under their rotting house? You couldn't very well spit out this rancid cake, only smile as you swallowed it by little, unhappy mouthfuls.

Mrs Jenkins said quite soon, 'I'll leave you to Viva, Maureen. I'm going down the road to look up a friend.' She gave her daughter a sideways look.

Was she so confident in the effect of the cake, so callous that she was leaving her daughter to accept full responsibility? And could Viva be such a perfidious friend?

Mrs Jenkins went out as she was, in her thin dank hair, easy cotton frock and feet bare except for the pink corn plaster.

While her mother was still within earshot, Viva explained, 'She's after the gasfitter, Bernie Horan. A fat lot of hope she's got of finding that one.'

'The cake . . .' Irene mumbled through her misery.

'Yair. Spit it out.' She offered a blue plastic bowl such as Mrs Bulpit kept her teeth in overnight. 'Isn't it poisonous! I couldn't warn yer.'

To take her mind off the cake, Irene asked, 'What were you going to show me, Viva? Something your father brought from Brazil—or was it Patagonia?'

'Both. I'll tell you. But you've *gotter* give me time. It's a secret I never thought of sharing with anybody else.'

She went to a cupboard and after fumbling round at the back brought out a polished wooden box inlaid with ivory, ebony, and turquoise chips. The turquoise might have been due to light or inspiration or the mystic state Viva had invoked earlier on.

'You don't miss a trick,' she said, still withholding the contents of the box. 'My father got it when he was a merchant seaman—while he was on a voyage to Brazil. He made this horseback journey into the interior through the jungle, along the banks of a great river. He was in such good favour with the Indians—who recognised him for what he was—that they made him a present of a talisman which he always kept in this box.'

Again in speaking of her father her voice took on the thrumming tone of a 'cello string.

Irritated by delay, Irene urged, 'Come on, let's have a look at it.' Mrs Jenkins might return too soon, or as a recurrence of unhappy nausea reminded, you might die of the grandmother's fatty cake.

Viva opened the lid of the box. Inside was a white satin square beautifully stitched with gold thread. On removal of the sheet a black object not much larger than a fist was revealed.

'You wouldn't think,' Viva said in an awful voice, 'that this could have ever been a human head.'

Irene did not stop to think because she immediately accepted the object as an addition to her private world. A few threads of coarse hair were still adhering to the little scalp, and from the chin the bristles of a beard, less like hair than fine wire. But it was the slits where eyes and mouth had been which provoked the deepest shiver.

Not to show Viva the extent of the impression the shrunken head had made on her, she asked as casually as she could, 'What does your mother think of it?'

'Says it gives her the creeps. She'd have thrown it out after my father left, if I hadn't told her it would probably come back—or revenge itself in some terrible way. So she lets it alone.'

'You're very lucky, to have it,' Irene said.

Gil Horsfall's stolen brooch was nothing to compare with Viva's talisman from the Brazilian jungle. She herself had nothing but memories, images, and the threads of words and phrases which were constantly sprouting in her.

'How does Patagonia come in?'

'That's where Carlos came from. He was a Patagonian Welshman.' Viva immediately replaced the satin sheet and snapped the lid of the box shut. 'They must never know at school,' she said, 'that I'm not like any normal Australian.'

Viva's confession was so strange and unexpected you forgot for a moment your own abnormality. When realisation that the condition of which she was alternately ashamed and proud was one that she had in common with Viva Irene felt resentful.

She pursed her mouth. 'I don't know that it's all that terrible—not like being a reffo,' she added to show her willingness to shoulder Viva's share of guilt.

'I often feel all mixed up,' Viva mumbled, quoting from a letter in a magazine Irene had found and read in Mrs Bulpit's lounge room.

Any insecurity and confusion of your own became in consequence a distinction Viva would not have known about.

'I think it's time I went,' Irene said soon after.

'Promise not to tell,' Viva called from the gate.

Not now that the secret had become more yours than Viva's.

Irene waved back. A scattering of bats had begun weaving their evening flight. On the sky line the image of the shrunken head hung more purposefully, it seemed. Aunt Cleonaki must surely have accepted the mystic head as she would have approved some miracle-working black Panayia made respectable by the rigid vestments of Orthodoxy.

The image of the head only dissolved as Mrs Jenkins was seen advancing up the road.

'I couldn't contact my friend,' she said with the composure of a lady returning from a visit to another. 'Any messages will have to keep.'

It seemed in no way unusual that she should be hatless, gloveless, and barefooted, except that stones had drawn blood and the plaster was missing from her corn.

'I wonder what nonsense that girl of mine's been telling you,' she said and laughed. 'About her father, I bet. That lousy bastard—she can't get over his disappearance. I could tell you—but won't . . .'

Her denture wobbled, and cracks were reappearing in her composure.

'Run along, dear,' she advised, 'It isn't safe for a young girl, so many undesirables around in wartime—in peace too, you've got to face it.'

Irene continued on her way to Cameron Street. She felt strangely protected by the image of the head which she had appropriated as her talisman, and for the moment at least, indifferent to people and events.

• • •

Not long after, it seemed, though in fact they were strung out on the thread of months, perhaps even years, three important events occurred to shatter Irene's sense of inviolability.

Event No 1

It was a steamy morning. You had gone down early, before the others were up, through the dark garden, to the sea wall. Everything dusty, or dank, or patent-leathery about the foliage had been exorcised by an influx of slow light. In the lower garden the hibiscus trumpets were expanding, and reaching upwards into what was not their native province, their pistils bejewelled with a glittering moisture along with the wings of big velvety butterflies. Their petals flapped through territory which normally belonged to moths and bats. The harbour had subsided this morning into a sheet of wet satin. Gulls had furled their harshness for the moment and were amiably afloat above their reflections. There was no reason why the city should ever catch fire again, as it had the evening Mamma sailed on the return voyage to Egypt and Greece.

No *reason*.

But you were suddenly sucked back through the sticky web of light and colour the garden the morning had become as though for some celebration you were forced up the paths breath grown furry one big hibiscus trumpet blinding with its scarlet as the cruel phonograph voice ground out of some still blurred dream or memory.

At the top of the path, beyond the Moreton Bay fig, the walls of the cubby in its branches mildewed and exhausted, the house had never looked so huge, while at the same time it appeared preparing to fall apart.

Something was happening. Someone had arrived. As you opened the screen door at the back, it hummed like a rusty hornet. From the stove a stink of spilt milk.

Mrs Bulpit's voice was rising. 'Too much happens. A person can't expect me to cope,' she moaned, 'not in my state of health.'

There was the undertone of a second voice.

'. . . *nobody* expects you to . . . my responsibility . . .' ending in a smoky cough which partly veiled the speaker's sex.

Gil was standing in the scullery. He was holding his case, ready to catch the bus for school, to arrive at the point where he ceases to know you. He has grown too fat? The cloth is tight round his buttocks. The hair he has begun growing on his thighs prickles like a dog's from whatever is happening. His face could have heard about a murder or a fire has broken out in one of these old wooden dry-rotten houses. His strong pimpling throat is again a little boy's. The adam's apple has been halted.

Out of sight Essie Bulpit is slopping over.

When Mrs Lockhart—you would like to see her as Aunt Alison—steps into view.

'Irene, dear—Eirene,' she makes this supreme concession, '. . . Mrs Bulpit and I think you'd better . . . Mr Harbord agrees to let you off school today.'

It is the sign for Gil to uproot himself. His larger-sized shoes (shoes have to be bought as you grow, though garments can wait till the old become indecent) are kicking out, to shake off something holding him back, or excrement of some kind. Has he kicked that hole in the screen door, or was it already there in the old rusty mesh? Get away any way up to the bus. There is no reason why he should stay to contract a disease from someone who has to be quarantined.

His leather is stamping on the cracked concrete path. Escaping. The bus is suddenly, all of it desirable, the pimply raucous street boys, Mr Burt's hands twisting the wheel, *wrestling*. Viva's fringe and smell, the smudgy faces and limp shopping bags of those who belong to a different life, in which the shortage or availability of things, together with their price, are both as important and out of date as weights and measures on the blackboard under Mr Manley's hands.

Anyway school is out for this morning, and you are looking at Aunt Ally's throat or cleavage in her bosom, the blackhead in it throbbing.

'Come into the lounge, Irene,' she said, 'there's something we must have a talk about.'

Do you smell? Or has somebody been reading your thoughts?

Essie Bulpit has prudently retreated to her bedroom. She has heard what Aunt Ally has to tell and wouldn't want to hear again, unless it was really interesting—or bad. Ally is looking so nervous, her glassy blue eyes avoiding her burnt skin hanging in more than usually pronounced rags, the thing she has to tell must be real bad. After she had hardly settled herself in a groaning of the Bulpit springs, and forced a fresh pack of cigarettes out of the carton corseting it, she can't postpone any longer.

So she started off. 'You can't expect only happiness, dear, out of life,' as if you didn't know, 'the blows will come as well. And what I have to tell you will probably be the greatest blow.'

Go on tell, tell, I can take it, because you have as good as told me.

'Wouldn't you like to come and sit beside me, dear?'

She holds out a hand, with its crummy rings, and the cigarette trembling between stained fingers. While you continue standing where you are. She will think you cold, but it's okay by Ally if you don't accept her invitation, her imitation of kindness, she doesn't go in for touching, or not more than can be helped.

'It's about your mum, darling.'

'I know.'

She looks put out, if not frightened. 'How did you know? Did somebody tell you?'

'No.'

How to tell Ally, who likes to live in her own car, driving round the bright Harbour bays, with her cigarettes and tissues, the boys' sports gear, and the wilting vegetables she has bought cheap, keeping all else at arm's length, unless the God she doesn't believe in gives her a motor accident, how to tell this aunt you are half moth that knows by downy instincts, half Attic rock that can withstand the Turk's scimitar.

'Well, if you claim to know,' she says rather angrily, aligning her big feet in their scuffed shoes in front of her on the Wilton carpet, 'it makes it easier for both of us. Though it doesn't seem natural. You *aren't natural*, Ireen.' The glassy eyes are back in true glaring form. 'To know that your mother is dead—and to feel nothing, it appears—you're just not an ordinary girl.'

'Where did she die? Greece?' It might after all become unbearable, you can feel your wiry legs bending, possibly giving.

'No, in Egypt—in Alexandria.'

'How?'

Facts are more in Ally's line. She lets out a raw, relieved cough, and a funnel of smoke.

'In a bombing raid. She and her friend—I forget his name—and a number of others must have died instantly, when the house they were visiting,' she coughed again, 'suffered a direct hit.'

She makes it sound as though it's in the newspapers. Only unknown people die. It suits both of you this way.

Oh no no it doesn't. You know about the other. Not from Mamma lying under Alexandrian rubble. But father murdered in his cell. Now Mamma has ended something. Greece—my heart—is dead.

Ally is extracting herself from a horrible situation and the groaning Bulpit sofa. 'I like to think you feel more than you let me see. And now to be practical—not to brood over what's happened and can't be undone—why don't we drive somewhere for the day.

Do a little shopping in the city en route. I'll buy you anything you have a fancy for—provided it's not too extravagant—in war time.'

Keep it light, bright, and inexpensive for poor old Ally.

'No.' It seems your voice will never learn to play along. 'I'd rather stay here.'

'What—with Mrs Bulpit? She's—in no fit state . . .'

'With nobody.'

Ally hunches her shoulders. Unnaturalness in others makes her look deformed.

When she has gone, after you hear her driving away, the room, this recent torture chamber, settles back into its normal dull shape. You go outside into the garden to regain your normal balance. But nothing will ever be the same.

'Eirene' is dead. I am Irene Ireen Reenie anything this Australian landscape dictates their voices expect. Not altogether. Little bits of 'Eirene' are still flapping torn and bloody where they have been ground into the broken concrete strewn along the sea wall amongst the gulls' scribble little spurts of knowledge will always intrude on what others are babbling about and on what I have learned to learn from blackboard and textbook, memory will always be bloodier than pinpricks the cruel tango we can't resist in any of its movements in the bilious Alexandrian *patisserie* in Attic dust in mountain snow my mouth is watery with what I must live and already know.

When will Gil come and I tell him about Mamma? Or does he already know—perhaps more than I? It will be a comfort—to watch his face—to touch his hand—if I dare.

The bus has passed. He hasn't come. Gone with Lockharts perhaps. Is he afraid of somebody who has been touched by death?

The Bulpit calls 'You two'll have to get your own tonight. I feel too sick. There's cold stuff in the flyproof.'

He comes in, throws his case in the corner.

'Walked back this evening. Exercise.'

He puts on his ugliest voice, flexes his muscles to demonstrate the virtue in exercise. He has grown some more, it seems, since morning. He disappears somewhere he doesn't want you to follow.

Much later he shows up and we stand together shivering gnawing at a couple of pork bones ('Mr Finlayson's favour') and swallowing a mess of cold bread pudding.

The night is a naked electric bulb.

'Did you hear about Mamma?'

You both shiver worse than ever pressed up against the table, its American cloth strewn with shavings of pork fat and grey gobbets of bread pudding.

'Yes, it was bad luck.' He has grown suddenly precise and English. 'Anyone can cop a bomb. If your name's on it. Nigel did.'

Gil has his own store of knowledge.

'She must have died instantly.' It's your newspaper voice, borrowed from old Ally Lockhart.

'Reckon the lot of them did.'

'Do you know who they were?'

'Bruce Lockhart says they were a mob of allied staff officers, who'd gone along to this fancy Gyppy *whorehouse*, when the bomb fell.' He began to laugh. 'Pinpointed, I'd say. Sounds like a great spy story.' His ugly laughter clattering against his man's teeth in a boy's mouth.

You long to kiss and heal his hateful mouth, return the beauty you know is there.

He has begun to see you. 'Sorry, Irene. You must be cut up about your mother.' Again the well-brought-up English boy. 'Ought to go to bed, oughtn't we?'

We are tramping in opposite directions. The same if you dared admit.

The same.

• • •

Event No 2

It happened in the holidays which made it in some respects easier.

Gil is out boating with Bruce and Keith. You are sitting at your table ruling the notebook you think of keeping as a diary—if you dare.

The boat heels as they jump from side to side indulging in that boring pastime sailing a boat. (Sails in the distance are a different matter). But hulking males. The hairy Lockharts. And GILBERT HORSFALL (you have already printed the name on a secret page of the diary you haven't begun to keep) in his imitation of the Lockharts. His hands have not lost their original shape.

The hand of Fatima on Arab houses to protect them against evil.

Most Greeks are hairy. There's no getting round that one 'Eirene'.

'Ireen?'

The Bulpit is calling from her room. We are all living in separate rooms. (The only shared moments are in the single room of the tree-house, and Essie thank God can't climb the ladder.)

'Okay, Mrs Bulpit, I'm *coming*.' Such a binding grind.

Essie is lying in her awful bed, which she shared with the W/O, and you with Mamma that first night. Enough associations to disassociate anyone for ever.

'What can I do for you, Mrs Bulpit?' Your hypocritical mini-voice.

'Re-fill the hotwater bottle, dear.'

On one of the steamy summer mornings.

It is so long since you looked out of yourself and saw Essie that doing so now is a shock. At the end of the arm dangles the slack hotwater bottle in its fluffy pink jacket. There is the smell of sick rubber. The thin arm suggests pelican bones. She is without her teeth, her yellow throat dangles and wobbles on the rumpled sheet, she has the pelican's not quite bird and not quite human eye.

'Yes, Mrs Bulpit. Don't worry. I'll fill the bottle.' Speaking like an adult.

You would have stayed boiling the kettle if the hotwater bottle in its pink jacket hadn't looked and felt like something fetched up out of Essie's insides.

'Thank you, dear—it's a comfort—to hold . . .'

When she has rolled round a bit in the bed, the contours of her slack body gurgling and subsiding, Essie says from out of her gums, 'I've always tried to do me duty, whatever it was. But there comes a time . . .'

If only she won't start slobbering. No slobber left perhaps, only those pelican bones and slack wobbly pouch.

'People think you're a fool today if you have your principles.' No longer human.

That black bead of the pelican's eye. You are the one will start slobbering. Oh God, to die without finding a duty. But what? Mamma thought she had one and let it down. Cleonaki had her duty to the Panayia and the Saints, the same wooden face in a change of robes. The old wrinkled voice reading from the Gospels. The classics too. *For what we may learn, though we may not approve, Eirinitsa, of the passions they illustrate.* So we read *Phèdre* aloud, and it is thrilling, no less in Cleonaki's crackling voice. . . . *de l'amour j'ai toutes les fureurs* . . . What has she known of the furies of love, this dusty voice, the face like an old, white wrinkled glove? Did Cleonaki tremble when she kissed the Archimandrite's hand. Or was it all ideas and tales?

'You love them and they let you know, more or less, you're a fool for doing so.' Again the voice of the pelican. 'Reg never understood duty—except to his men, the C.O., and the customers after we opened the pub in Sydney. Well, it was a duty—a man's duty. I suppose you'd call it. A woman's is different.'

'Better not tire yourself Mrs Bulpit. You're ill. I advise you to relax.' In extremis, yes, extremis, you are copying Aunt Alison.

Thank God a car is pulling up outside. A visitor—a tradesman—*anybody*.

It is Aunt Alison's trampling feet her voice pushing the way into the room, to Mrs Bulpit's dreadful rumpled bedside. She doesn't notice a mere niece, there is no good reason why she should.

'The ambulance will be here any moment now, Mrs Bulpit. You have no need to worry.' Mrs Lockhart even throws in a 'dear' for somebody who was never her friend. Aunt Alison's idea of doing her duty.

'I was always a worrier. That's my trouble,' Essie replies in a calm voice. 'Has the gentleman been informed—who will act as Gilbert's guardian? The Colonel would never forgive me . . .'

'The Colonel—nobody need worry. Mr Stallybrass is an accountant—a correct and honourable man.'

Aunt Alison is sweating in the untanned rims to her glassy eyes. Once the ambulance has come she may never forgive Essie for calling on her to do her duty.

The ambulance men stumble a lot. They are old, one fat and puffing, one thin and suppressed. The strong and young are away at the war. But these do their duty. They call Essie 'love'. She takes it all for granted. Aunt Alison drags on another cigarette as one of Essie's sheets forms round her ankles.

The pelican bones, the hotwater bottle, are more than you can bear. You run out, vomit beside the back steps, fall into the leaf mould, amongst the spiders, the ants, the centipedes, and many other mysteries crushing and crushed.

Aunt Alison comes out presently and calls, 'Irene? I've got to follow on to the hospital. Back later. Tell that Horsfall boy his guardian will be fetching him. He must pack his things. You, too.'

Finally you are alone in the garden. As you raise your head, there is a long silver thread connecting your chin with the earth on which you have been lying.

Packing our things.

They don't amount to much more than what you came in with. Aunt Alison and Mrs Bulpit have used the war as an excuse for not buying 'a lot of expensive clothes you'll grow out of next month.' It saved them the trouble. And was less to pack now thank God. Writing paper, droring paper. The diary you will begin to write when you have the time and courage, and Gil won't be in the next room. This naked sixpenny exercise book. And books, heavy to carry, in a port, dirty old, inky old school texts. *I love a sunburnt country*—not today—or will you ever? No country where the memories are all burnt into you, together with the secret pockets you are exploring every day in the present, in the depths of your mind. *Selected Poems of Lord Byron.* Tell him found a thing or two yourself. You cannot carve poems about Greece in marble. Greece shifts as you watch, like weather, dust, water.

Snaps. Nothing of Papa, Mamma, Cleonaki, Evthymia. We left in too much of a hurry and Mamma says, 'Photographs become in time so much sentimental trash.' Instead a lot of silly school groups. Kids alone or in couples. Ireen, Lily and Eva having it off with the camera. Only one of 'Gilbert Horsfall' (signed on the back). Essie Bulpit took it with her Kodak just as he moved. Gil is standing, a silver blur, against the sea wall. Like to have a good one—or three, or four.

This snap is something, perhaps it is even more so than Gil. Because you persuaded Viva to take her father's Brazilian jungle head from out of its inlaid box and hold it in a good light to photo. Viva does not know whether to look sideways at the head, or squint into the sun and the camera. The head is cupped against her broad white hand and not quite recognisable. If you didn't know. If it hadn't become your talisman.

Gil comes in.

'Done your packing?'

'Yes. Are you sure this accountant bloke will come tonight?'

'That's what she said.'

'It's pretty sudden.'

'Illness can be sudden.' Sounds too prim, prissy. 'Anyway she's gone to hospital. She's pretty crook.'

'Might die.'

'Oh no, I don't think she'll die.' When this is exactly what you are expecting and fearing another chapter ending in death.

'What's this?' he asks, taking up the snap of Viva holding the shrunken head.

You tell, not all of it, now that this black object, sacred after its fashion, has become your talisman.

'Could be a fake.' He throws it back on the table where you have been going through the snaps.

'Why does everything have to be a fake?'

'A lot is.' He is looking distracted from all that is happening. His nostrils are perfect, like one of the poems Lord Byron carved on marble.

You could whimper, but instead 'What did you do with that brooch?'

'Oh . . .' You might have hit him the way he jumps. 'Threw it away. What would I do with a bloody brooch?

'Could have given it to me. I could have worn it.'

'Well, I didn't. See? Wouldn't have wanted you to wear the brooch. They might think I was on with you.'

You can both have a laugh at that.

Less laughter as the evening deepens. Neither of you knows whether you want to be apart or together, in the house, or the garden. You roam around and it is mostly, at last, apart.

You would have to be the one passing by the phone when it rings.

Ally's voice, darker and furrier than normal. '. . . still at the hospital, Irene . . . very sick . . . she has *no-one* . . . Who has? . . . Two big children . . . learn to cope with a crisis . . .' Ally must have sloshed down a couple of drinks. '. . . Keep you up to date. Bye dear.' Crump.

O my uncle—God save us!

Gil breaks in. 'Why doesn't this Stallybrass chap come?' His voice has climbed back to his present physical height, out of its Australian slump and sludge, back to its pure Englishness, the tips of his teeth transparent behind his parted lips.

'Search *me*. He's held up.'

With no-one in the room to accuse, Gilbert Horsfall would like to hold me responsible. He flops down on one of Essie's protesting chairs, his long thighs, his long hands, a face which doesn't bear looking at, no part of him accommodated to the Australian light, air, his skin has only reached a compromise with the Australian sun. Or anyone.

Nobody thinks of whether there is anything to eat.

'Going to lie down.' You are soon entombed on the ottoman, amongst the junk furniture Essie has hoarded, and her own dummy, its bosom full of death murmurs.

From the sound of things, Gil must have thrown himself on the narrow bed under the slanting, blown-up portrait of the W/O.

The telephone rings, but peters out in a couple of idiotic tinkles.

I am the idiot born to die sitting upright on the edge of this tomb-bed my mouth open but paralysed.

I am running a great distance.

We bump into each other halfway there. I can feel the veins in his long arms as we hold each other in part of the immense darkness. Who is leading who in this *cruel tango*?

Who who who on the honeycomb of this narrow stretcher is holding who.

I am holding his head.

Is Gil crying or are our mouths watering together as he fingers only part of me a pimple to his finger,

'Noooh . . .'

'Go on, Reenee . . .'

'Noh!'

His sharp nail is at odds with his dreamy mouth.

If I gave in and had a baby it would be less than this head I am holding protecting the soft jumping in a sleeping body the very first time I have held someone asleep.

All voices Mamma Cleonaki Essie Ally are united with the warning gong of daylight. And the unknown voice.

'Anybody there?' Rattling the rusty catch, the whole frame of the screen door:

Mr Stallybrass the accountant?

As we brush aside the untidiness of sleep, each dazed gummy face is taking possession of itself. Sleep has bruised us.

It is Gil who is being called on to exercise authority, which he does while buttoning up, thumping first across lino, then the splintery grey boards of the back veranda, 'Coming, mister—sir . . . Mr Stallybrass?'

'Couldn't make it last night. Early morning's the next best thing.'

Gil grunting.

'Fetch your traps. I've got the vehicle waiting.' Must want to get away quick as possible.

From the kitchen shadows you can watch Mr Stallybrass holding the screen door open for the quick exit of his new charge. Extracting this boy from a difficult situation and his own failure to do his duty is obviously child's play to anyone of the accountant's experience. His hands with the well-trimmed nails, the wristwatch and the signet ring, are firm, and fairly muscular. A bald head, gold-rimmed specs, and rather large spaced teeth, help increase the gloss and confidence of his smiles. There is no evidence that he has seen you, but he must have by now.

Gil comes carrying the two overloaded ports. The weight and his attempt at haste make him less manly than he would like to appear. His shoulders are hunched, his ribs visible inside the summer shirt. Round his neck he has attached his football boots by joined strings. ('Hate this bloody football, but if you don't go along with it they'll say you're a poofter.') The boots make an almost jeering sound as they thump his chest.

You are forced out at last from the building by wanting to do, or say something—but what?

'A girl . . .'

The accountant's murmur is too vague, little more than a sigh, to convey either censure or approval. His smile remains in position probably out of habit.

Gil only grunts as he starts the struggle up the hill to the gate. Mr Stallybrass makes a move to help with one of the ports, then thinks better of it.

You run out after them, on bare feet over the chunks of broken concrete. The others must have heard, but Gil makes no sign of knowing you are there, while every one of the few hairs left to Mr Stallybrass between his bald dome and his starched collar is bristling with hirsuteness. It makes you feel quite naked inside your cotton frock.

Confrontation is avoided by arrival of the Lockhart Chev. Aunt Alison is unfolding as she drags herself out. She looks older, thinner than the day before. The rags of her burnt face are almost purple over white. She must have run short of cigarettes.

'Alison Lockhart,' she explains briefly. 'Mrs Bulpit will have mentioned . . .'

Faced with Mrs Lockhart, Mr Stallybrass has lost a good deal of his confidence.

'Of course, yes.'

'I went with her to the hospital—spent most of the night there in fact.'

'I hope . . . ?'

'She died early this morning . . .'

'Oh dear!' Though his smile lingers, the accountant's hand falters as he unlocks the Daimler's boot.

Too much is happening at once. Aunt Alison has gashed her hand on the rusty gate. She watches the blood trickle down over the stains of nicotine. Gil is raising his luggage, packing it inside the shining car. Mr Stallybrass fears the boy may have grazed its precious paint.

The football boots are bumping around foolishly on their string as this long, painfully breathing form fits itself into the passenger seat.

Ignoring the unexplained barefoot girl, Mr Stallybrass bows at Mrs Lockhart, who does not return the civility. She is winding a dirty handkerchief round her bleeding finger.

The accountant drives smoothly off. Seated beside him, re-arranging the football boots Gilbert Horsfall does not look back.

How are you to take all these people, this coming and going, and Essie's death, when it is Gil who has died?

Perhaps he looked back once after your back was turned to exchange a secret smile, and because your face wasn't there to receive it, would imagine you have given him up.

'Come on, Ireen,' Aunt Ally calls. 'There's a hell of a lot to get through.'

She has developed a limp, perhaps out of sympathy with the finger, or she may have really fallen down on her way here from the hospital.

It doesn't stop her stamping through the house, slamming, locking windows (she has cracked a pane in one).

'What are we supposed to do, Aunt Ally.'

'Tidy up. Sort things out. Well, I couldn't bear it—not today.'

It is Essie's bedroom which has made her decide—the smell of sickness, stale powder, the big unmade bed—the lot.

'Not today. I'd fetch up.'

You are following her out to the tune of keys, only remembering at the back door.

'We're forgetting my possessions, Aunt Ally.' She can't stop hooting! 'Aren't you old-fashioned! Your possessions! You poor dear!'

She helps you up the slope with what there is. She has lost her limp. But her breath is terrible, a long sweet smoky blast.

'Your possessions!' as she drives snorting away.

There is all the usual trash in the Chev, along with a new sound, of an empty gin bottle rolling around on the floor at the back.

'You must wonder why I didn't come for you last night. You're too young. It's something you wouldn't understand. What that poor devil of a frightful female did to me. So I had a few drinks and drove around. You wouldn't understand. Couldn't creep into my *house*. People asleep. So I drove. Night's perhaps the best part of life—if you're on your own—and have a car.'

She almost runs off the road making the turn at this culvert, but it doesn't seem to matter much.

'Shall I be able to go back sometimes to the garden?'

'If you *want* to—anyway till the house is sold. Don't expect the new owner would want a stray girl nosing round his property,' Aunt Ally beeps. '*Garden*—I'd call it a wilderness.'

On every side—a country of lantana and feral cats.

'Do you have the accountant's address?'

'His *office* address. She forced it on me on account of the boy. But there's no reason why I should have any traffic with that *person*—in his bleeding Daimler—now that Gil-bert has been disposed of.'

We drive on towards the house in which my 'aunt' and my 'cousins' live. It's listed under the name of 'Harold Lockhart' (in the telephone directory). Harold felt even less an uncle than the boys are cousins, or Ally except at odd moments, an aunt. If you could have your own way, you wouldn't want to meet anyone else, related or unrelated, ever . . .

Event No 3

The move to Lockharts' was perhaps an even greater event than Nos 1 and 2 though each a vicious and unexpected blow, Mamma's death, which was also the death of Papa's ideal, then on top of it Essie's illness, the end of the garden, and Gil Horsfall's back as he was driven off. The move to Lockharts' was linked with education, which made it that much more formidable. All these boys talking about exams and what they would be doing in the future. Harold Lockhart ('never call me "uncle", Irene') at work in the Department of Education. All of it meant that you were being *formed*, that any part of Eirene Sklavos which survived, must exist only in the secret poetic world of dream and memory. Well, it has been like this already, but without the same brutal onslaught from boys and a Public Service uncle all geared to what most adults refer to as life. At Lockharts' you are formally Eirene Sklavos, in their eyes, if they ever take a look at you.

It must be said for Harold that he calls you 'Irene' not 'Ireen', in his soft, what passes for educated voice. Books and music have made him persuasive. He paints a little at the week-end—what he calls 'mood painting'. There is nothing outwardly brutal about Harold. He is too soft-spoken, soft silvery hair. A gentle man. Except when he remembers to look at you, and something happens to the corners of his mouth, pleating, moistening, and his eyes of that lovely soft silvery blue, compared with Alison's harsh glare, suddenly harden. Then you know that Harold is one of those people who know what they want. There's nothing wrong with that of course. If only you did.

There is a great shuffle round at Lockharts' following your unexpected, unwanted arrival. There is the question of rooms. Bruce and Keith, they are big, each has one of his own. Bob and Lex, the freckled, pig-rooting brumbies from back of the class, they already share. It is the little ones Col and Wal who suffer, they are banished to a sleep-out, and you will suffer accordingly in what was once their nice room, where their gear and toys continue to be stored. They are free to run in and fetch what they need, giggling as if they had found you naked. Throwdowns and stink bombs are what they see as the best jokes. And once an imitation dog turd.

Ignore. There is a drawer in which you can lock the diary you haven't yet begun to write. A wonder the key has survived Col and Wal.

There is the Saturday arvo they are all going to the cricket match. You are planning to say you don't feel well. Will Alison fall for it? Or will she *tot* up and find it's too soon after last time.

What she says is, 'It'll do you good. Take you out of yourself, mix with others in the fresh air. You're becoming *morbid*, Ireen.'

Actually she mustn't believe any of this, driving round by herself in her smelly old car, getting sloshed on gin alone at night—'the best part of life'. But because she is officially on the parents' side she goes along with what is supposed to be.

'You're not sickening for something, are you?' Your aunt looks genuinely anxious for a moment, as though she couldn't bear it if somebody else is preparing to die.

'NO.'

The truth was you were longing to indulge in the luxury of lying on the bed in full health, thinking and dreaming, then after their departure has stopped rocking the house, and it has subsided into its natural shape, to get up and take a look in the glass at this new person you are becoming, perhaps even write about it in the clean locked-up diary, all those threads of words and thoughts sprouting out of a pen.

Everything happens, as far as you can tell, according to plan. The silence is as soothing as lanoline on a sore place. A twig falls. Birds pick at an Australian silence without tearing it apart. Except the kookaburra, which is either in league with humans, or else laughing at them.

The kookaburra is the counterpart of this counterpane, as silence is to lanoline. You could lie here all afternoon rubbing your back your arms your whole body against this rough bedspread, surrounded by a silence through which twigs feathers can be heard falling. Except you are forced up by a shortening of time, it is never yours for long enough, to look in the mirror or unlock the drawers which contain secrets.

The mirror makes you look a guilty thief. In this seersucker *bolero*, it is called, and matching skirt, the white blouse. If it wasn't for your Greek skin and a spot you have rubbed too hard at on your chin, you might compete in the Australian Pretty Girl Stakes. But you will always look too black—and too guilty—nobody wins who has these fatal flaws. The plait is gone. '. . . advise you to cut off, long hair today makes a girl look frowsy, the "Ambleside" hat is frumpish enough without a lot of hot, heavy hair, hanging down or shoved up . . . have them cut it off . . . *cut* . . . CUT . . .'

Ally would never know what it is to have your plait cut off. She knows what goes. However, up the line at Ambleside three more weeks till term. Miss Hammersley is head.

Will Col and Wal find out this one drawer is locked, and force it? Better not keep a diary after all, have foreign eyes dirty its pages with sniggers. This guilty mirror is against all such foolishness.

Jan 1943

Well, I've got down to it—scribble—scribble. The relief. So much I've always wanted to say in any language new or old—στη γλώσσα μου, whichever that is.

Most since Gil was driven off in the accountant's car.

Asked Aunt Ally, 'Where is Gil living now?' She pursed up and answered, 'With his guardian, I presume.'

'But where?'

'Oh somewhere—in Vaucluse.' Her lips could barely speak the word.

'Where is that?' as though you didn't know.

'Somewhere out—the other side of the Bridge.' Her teeth have had enough of whereabouts.

In Sydney, it seems, a bridge does not bridge, it separates.

'What will happen to him now? Where will he be going to school?'

'At some so-called *public* school, SAGS I'm told. I couldn't care. He's no responsibility of mine.'

She closes the matter with a snap.

Gil will become a product of the Sydney Anglican Grammar School while I am to be ironed out up the line by Miss Hammersley of 'Ambleside'. Worlds between us, as Aunt Ally, I suspect, wishes.

What do they want to do with us? Do they really care? Responsibilities. I think Ally hates me at times because I am Mamma's child. Gerry escaped, married a commo, and had affairs with men. I hate men! Those *kind* army officers, the Greek Axiomatic dancing with Mamma in the *patisserie*, his badly fitting trousers, Mr Harbord exchanging looks with Mrs Lockhart, Harold 'never call me uncle', Bruce and Keith behaving like the men they haven't yet become.

Gilbert Horsfall is another pretender.

At his best he is something else, almost part of myself, the one I have shared secrets with, the *pneuma* I could not explain, but which he must understand, from what I know of his best moments, not the braying jackass in him.

If I could choose I would shut myself with Gil in the tree-house above the precipice in Cameron Street, floating, and the world could explode around us . . .

It nearly did day before yesterday. While I am writing I hear footsteps approaching through the house I thought mine for at least one afternoon. Put away your diary. I couldn't. I was paralysed. Anyway what did it matter? If it was one of the murderers you hear about? Or some GI. Those who murder or rape don't take any interest in a diary.

Then when the figure appears in the doorway it is my non-uncle, Harold Lockhart. 'Did I give you a fright?' he asked. 'No,' I lied, 'only I thought everyone had gone to the cricket match.' He said he had stayed behind to do a bit of painting. Sport is for morons, except you've got to play it to get on.

He pulled up a chair and sat down beside me at the desk, asked me what I was writing. I told him I was making notes for a school essay we had been asked to write. On what theme? How I see myself. That should be interesting, when you show us nothing of yourself, Irene, how you think or feel, anyone would postulate that you don't care for us. His voice dried up. He hummed a bit. He must have washed his hair. It had never looked so silvery, it sent out little waves of brilliantine. How is it, he asked, you're writing this essay when you're leaving the local school and starting next term at Ambleside? I was dripping by now, choking, what with Harold's hair and my own stupidity. When I thought to say, with my last gasp, that's right, but it will come in useful sooner or later, it's the sort of thing they ask you to write.

Luckily Harold did not seem all that interested in the 'notes for an essay'. His mouth was pleating and moistening at the corners as I had seen it before. 'Perhaps you have a literary talent,' he said, his eyes vague if they hadn't been concentrated on some intention which made him both sad and, yes, cruel. As concentration increased I was able to slip the diary into the drawer. He did not notice. He was drawing me between his knees. I have never fainted, almost once when Evthymia took me to Kapnikarea on Holy Friday and we kissed the face of the Panayia, now again I was on the point of fainting, what with the floating hair, the pressure of his thighs, and a thrumming sound from inside his shirt. Till I noticed the red lobes to his ears, and a razor nick he had made shaving the cleft in his chin. I despised myself more than I hated Harold.

While taking my head in his hands he is mumbling, 'Always so clean and neat, Irene, there's nothing like sluttishness to put a man off, when he has spent his life aspiring after perfection.' The hands were tightening on my head, the thighs drawing me close to him, the mouth opening, glistening, like a sleepy monster roused by a lone sprat behind the glass of an aquarium. I might have succumbed to this dangerously luscious anenome if it hadn't been for the smell of turps which had begun to drown the beautiful silvery perfume drifting out of recently shampooed hair. Behind the helmet in which his hands were encasing my head, a harsh halo of turps had almost completely taken over.

It gave me the opportunity to gasp, what were you painting—Harold?

He postponed his meal. Perhaps wondering whether the sprat was a bigger fish than he had bargained for, the silvery blue of the eyes became dazzling underwater spotlights.

'The movement of forms,' he told me 'through space by natural reaction, I mean nothing can resist nature's will though it may not be immediately visible to the obtuse human eye.'

Harold's inhuman eye was obviously daring me to resist.

'I always fail in what I set out to do,' his chest twangled despairingly 'and cannot persuade myself, like some artists, that truth lies in failure and the unknowable.'

He suddenly bends, and sticks the thin tip of a tongue which a moment before had been broad and furry, into my right ear, almost as deep as the drum it sounded at the moment of penetration.

'Do you understand, darling?' he laughs, 'I bet you do.'

'I would like to draw you Irene, on your bed—without your clothes—charming though they are.'

Without waiting for an answer, he picked me up and dumped me on the bed, and started arranging pillows, and arranging, and from there might have begun tearing at my clothes as though they were the wrapping of a parcel which prevented him getting at its contents quick enough.

When I've got to know you. Got your form and texture by heart I mean—I think we'll have a cat to elongate beside you, a big blue Persian with angry eyes and pink tongue.

It gave me my opportunity.

'I don't think Aunt Alison likes them. I don't think I do either. They make me itch and sneeze.'

'I knew it! You're turning out to be a dreary Philistine like all the others—and your Greek skin offers enormous tonal difficulties beside the blue cat I visualise.'

Outside, the kookaburra is tearing the garden apart. A cloud of finches and wrens are shedding their breast feathers as they beat against the glass.

'Let me see your nipples at least.'

Harold's hands which I had thought soft and pink are as hard and dry as turpentine has made them, with soot in the cracks.

I might have lost, knotting with those hard hands, if a worse clatter had not set up, competing with the kookaburra. I realised it was Alison, those scuffed brogues marching through her house.

Harold breathed, Oh Lord, and slithered quietly in the opposite direction, into the garden, only upsetting a garbage bin.

'Ireen?' Alison calls. 'Where are you?' and on charging through the doorway of my room, 'What are you doing?'

'Thinking.'

She was looking like a thin hen somebody with evil intentions had been chasing through the heat.

'Not very healthy, lying on your bed, on a fine afternoon.'

It was Alison who was looking unhealthy.

'Who won the match?'

'It isn't over. I left because I have a migraine coming on. The Parmores will bring the little ones back. The men can look after themselves.'

Apparently satisfied nobody else was in ill health, she went stamping out to the bathroom. 'Cricket!' she moaned, tablets rattling like dice in a tumbler, till a slosh of water silenced them.

'I don't expect somebody kind would like to make me a cup of tea,' she called back.

'That's just what I'm doing. Or at any rate I've put the kettle on.' It was Harold in the kitchen.

Ally could not have known what to answer. So I left them to their shared silence, or the argument they were brewing for when the kettle blew its whistle. I went into the garden.

This sad, sandy patch, all clothesline and failed vegetables, lacy cabbages, scribbley peas, rambling pumpkins. In Australia it is virtuous to grow your own vegetables while conning the greengrocer into selling you his wilting varieties cheap. The Lockhart garden is full of Ally's failures—and Harold's avoidances. And birds which nobody notices as they knock off the grubs Ally's vegetable ventures encourage. And cats—here for the birds, and more particularly, the overturned garbage bins—toms with swollen cheeks growling over chop-bones. Harold does not recognise cats, unless the aesthetic ones with tonal values. Ally sees them only when she drives past in her old car through a loneliness of lantana scrub.

Does Ally's car correspond to the tree-house Gil and I built and left behind. No, we didn't. We were only forced.

One of the predatory cats stalked across the scuffed sandy 'lawn' flicking an angry tail. She sat for a moment preening herself with a licked paw. I should not have dismissed cats in my conversation with Harold, saying they made me sneeze and itch. A handy lie—I have never *known* a cat. But would like to. I feel very close to them. I would love to stroke a cat's fur, from its bat's ears down to the tip of its snake's tail. Cleonaki would not have permitted an animal.

After she had done her face, (this slinky tortoise-shell could only have been a female—no swollen-cheeked, moth-eaten tom) she loped swiftly across the lawn into the lacy cabbages, and re-appeared in exit over the grey paling fence.

Almost at once the back door whammed. Harold, too, was making an exit. Where the lovely tortoise-shell loped, Harold stalked while hoping any observer might see it as a normal walk. Harold was taking the shortcut through a gap in the fence to the track which leads to the ferry. As he crossed the lawn I might not have existed. He looked through me, dismissing an experience which had not turned out the way he would have had it go. Only for an instant the eyes turned on, and you felt he might be saving you up for the future. Squeezing sideways through the gap in the grey palings (the stomach would only just make it) a shred of the exquisitely tonal gear was left behind on a rusty nail. The last of Harold drifted back as a muttered, 'Fuck.'

There was nothing to keep me, so I went back inside.

Ally called, 'Who's that?' and at once more hopefully, 'Is it Ireen?'

She was stretched out on her bed in her slip, a strip of wetted lint covering her eyes. Her temporary blindness should have made it easier to face her. But I felt guilty. It wasn't only for Harold's behaviour, and her relationship with my mother, it was for the whole undisguised shambles of Ally Lockhart in an old beige slip: the bruises on her shins, the thin strips of what had been breasts, the flaking lips in a face the weather had roughed and reddened. I have never stroked a cat. I should have been able to stroke my aunt if I hadn't felt so paralysed. At least she would have hated it (or so I think), and that let me off a little of my guilt.

Perhaps it was from not being able to see me that she became more confidential than ever in the past. What she resented most was callousness in human beings, by which she meant men—husbands. She went so far as to name him. Men's bodies last better than women's and husbands take advantage of it.

'I don't know why I'm telling you this,' she said. 'A child. But children, specially you, Ireen—know more today—too much—and at the same time not enough. You can't—the experience of life. I wish I had had a *girl* child . . .' After letting you see everything to put you off womanhood. But wanted you to share her suffering. 'Those boys of mine will grow into men and despise me for being old, ugly, and their slave. Sometimes I think I'd rather have a poof. Might too. Good God, no. I can't *possibly*.'

Presently we hear the little ones clattering in from the street. Ally's back arches on the bed and she tears the bandage off her eyes. 'What if the Parmores? That would be the last straw! No, Col and Wal will have given them enough. And they wouldn't want to face the boring mother . . .' So she sinks back. 'Be a darling, Ireen, and feed them. You're so capable . . .' she sighs.

Fortunately Col and Wal are still munching popcorn and sucking lollies. They want nothing. Hardly notice you are there. Run into what was once their room, to fetch a few toys. You hear the door slam in the writing table. As you go in to protect your secrets, the key tinkles on the floorboards.

Col asks, clutching his Donald Duck, 'What are you always writing, Reenee? Is it a story?'

'Yes, a story.'

Wal asks 'What about, Reen?'

'The lot of us.'

They have a giggle.

'Will you read it to us?'

'No need.'

More giggles as they run out to the veranda, Wal scattering bits of his meccano set.

Tonight I am the meccano set no-one will ever put together, even if all the bits are there.

Whatever got into you to keep a diary. Safer to share your secrets with a mirror. Shan't write any more. Ought to destroy it but think of all those little white moths taking wing, spreading the news. Burn it? Under the wad of tinkling carbon the core of the matter will lie waiting to be read. Steamy emotions are difficult to kindle. You have strung the key to the drawer on a chain, and wear it round your neck. Even this is dangerous.

'Ah, keepsakes,' Harold says at breakfast in the toneless voice with which he clothes his most feeling censure. 'I wonder *whose* snap has pride of place in Irene's locket.'

Bruce sniggers, 'Lionel Manley perhaps!'

Keith comes in with 'Lionel Manley? You don't say! There's a fair few of the girls have crushes on Lionel the Lily. You'd be surprised. Hot or frigid, it don't make no difference!'

Harold speculates with dead indifference, 'To which category I wonder, does our Irene belong?'

Bruce says you are a dark horse, no-one has found out yet, unless it's . . .

Just then her aunt appears with another dish of snags to appease her men.

'Oh Ireen's the passionate type like me. Aren't you, darl?' Ally gushes.

Everybody joins in the laugh then the boys settle down to wrapping their teeth round food, their lips soon as greasy as sausage skins, bloodied with tomato sauce.

But whose face would Bruce consider you might be wearing in the 'locket'?

Bruce and Keith are growing at the same rate as Gilbert Horsfall—or as Gil was when you last saw him. The Lockhart brothers are growing hairier every day. If ever at table Bruce lays his arm alongside yours it prickles like horsehair in some old burst mattress.

On these occasions his breathing grows more noticeable. He says he'll take you for a drive riding pillion when he gets that motorbike—'if you're not afraid.' You aren't because it's likely to be some way off. He is saving money from the jobs he does at week-ends and in the holidays when the climate doesn't damp his enthusiasm. Yes I think I'm safe from Bruce (or 'Bruise' as they pronounce it.)

It is Bruce who is bringing you this letter on the last Tuesday before term starts at 'Ambleside'. Know it as Tuesday. You will always remember it as Tuesday because this is the first letter you ever received with an Australian stamp on it, and Ally has finally bought you the uniform for the next terrifying phase of life in an Australian school.

The letter itself is frightening enough—'Bruise' has been up to the box. He advances into the back yard holding the envelope by a corner. You turn to face him.

'A formal letter for Miss Irene Sklavos.'

He minces towards me. His attempt at a refined accent, and the hairy wrist with its metal watchband as he jiggles the letter under my nose is meant to make the situation humiliating. The key on its chain lies cold between your painful breasts. Yes, you are humiliated.

If he leaves you to the letter it doesn't mean he isn't watching from inside the house. They are all watching, Alison and Harold for once united in boring into the contents of the envelope.

Kyrie eleison amongst the fretted cabbage leaves and silver snail tracks. Dragging at the corner of the envelope you make this prayer of joy and fear, crumbling into the Greek reffo you will always be.

The last must be first

Just a line from your fellow reffo

Gil

Doxa to Theo for these palpitations, this elevation, under the empty clothesline tingling with its droplets of moisture.

Dear Eirene (dear Gil)

I wonder how you are getting on since I left Neutral Bay. Isn't that Neutral the biggest laugh in war or peace? I would love to see you but our ways lie apart in life and schools. I am starting term at this Churchy Grammar School for boys, and you I hear are bound for 'Ambleside' and Miss Hammersley. I can only say good luck to us, mate.

I often think about us Reen—and the treehouse, the bloody cubby—you sitting on the upright Arnotts biscuit tin like it was your inherited throne. Perhaps it was. From all this we can only meet again.

Sorry my typing isn't all it ought to be. Fiona is letting me use her machine—so as Lockharts won't swoop in and recognise my writing. Fiona (Cutlack) is Mrs Stally's niece who lives here too. Vaucluse isn't all that bad—if not our sort of country Reen. What is, I'd like to know, outside the big fig tree in Cameron Street. Old Stally is the silliest bugger you ever had to put up with. You wonder anyone's accounts come right. Mrs S. is an invalid. Sundays we eat lunch at the Royal Sydney Golf Club. A lot of congealed custard and Stallybrasses galore. Fiona is the best of them. She's learning touchtyping, so as she can take a job till she marries—if the war doesn't last forever, if it does she'll go into the WRANS, she reckons the hats will suit her best.

Oh Jesus, the fucking war. Perhaps I should skip the school bit and join up. My dad ought to approve, if they ever approve of anything. Get killed like poor old Nigel. Don't think anything will kill Horsfall or if it does I'll come back to haunt the places we've been together.

Fiona says that most of what I say is pure bullsh. Hope you don't think the same, Reen, of what I sincerely feel

This FIONA is probably right . . .

Just a line from your fellow reffo

Gil

What to do with the letter? Stick it down your front with the key, if they won't hear the key beating against the envelope, if their long distance eyes haven't already read the message?

By the time you go in they have decided on their line of attack. Bruce gazing at the fly-specks on the ceiling, Keith his lids lowered, thick lips still greasy from breakfast trembling with amusement and the comb-and-paper tune he is humming. Ally has chosen a fit of busyness, scraping plates and jostling cups on saucers, to disguise her thoughts and intentions.

Only Harold expresses his disapproval in words. 'Hope it was good news, Irene. Or perhaps it was only a business letter.'

The secret we share gives his interest a sting which the others cannot feel.

'No. It's a letter from a friend.' My reply as flat as his enquiry.

'Glad you have friends around.' His low voice vibrates in a way which might reach deep inside someone who meets him for the first time at the Quay or on the ferry.

The ears of the others are pricking of course. To know who Reen's friend could possibly be. Your nostrils are pinched as you enjoy a twinge of evil in yourself. You could have stuck a pin in any of them as Viva stuck the pin in your arm that first day at school and seemed to grow hypnotised by the pinprick of blood.

Unable to solve a mystery, they go their different ways, and you are left with the ballooning melancholy which comes with the prospect of this new important school. Even the 'Ambleside' uniform has a smell of importance which warns off a black reffo Greek.

Would like to have another read of the letter, only Alison Lockhart reappears. Her face tells that she would like to have an intimate talk now that you are alone in the house. She accepts you as a woman, no longer the unwanted child-niece, because she wants to unload some of her own unhappiness.

'You will always be frank with me, dear—I hope —how can we trust each other if you aren't?'

Poor old Alison makes you feel happy by comparison—not to say dishonest. Has she guessed perhaps, and only wants it confirmed. She ought to know. It takes a very short time to find out all there is to know about Harold. If you could tell her that you are her ally, that Gil is your friend, as pure a secret as Harold is a dirty one. But secrets, whether pure or dirty, are for some people difficult to share.

Her aunt is off at a tangent. 'What I am afraid of,' she tears out a tissue, a box of which she keeps handy in every room, 'is that when you go to this school—up the line—other girls—their parents—will take you up, and from beginning to accept you as my own daughter, I shall—well, I shall never see you.'

It could be genuine, except that the sniffles and the Kleenex seemed to create a drama, an incestuous one at that, if Ally is my mother and Harold my would-be seducer.

You are trying not to laugh.

'What is it?'

'I was thinking of the Greek Tragedies.'

'I can't see any connection,' she says rolling the Kleenex into a ball, and throwing it in the waste paper basket. 'This is Australia and although you are a Greek, we thought—wrong or right—you had started seeing yourself as an Australian.'

It is too much.

'I don't know what I am. I don't want anyone

to—*take me up*. I only want to be left alone—to be myself—when I find out what that is.'

Ally is embarrassed by turning on emotion in somebody else. But she asked for it.

'How you exaggerate, Ireen. I do hope you won't blow your top like this at "Ambleside", and disgrace us all.'

Embarrassment gets rid of Alison. So at least you are alone, to think your own thoughts, if not to discover what you are.

The aunt can be heard driving off safe in her scungy old car, with its cigarettes and box of travelling tissues.

Alison had driven you up to the interview with Miss Hammersley. If you were accepted the 'principal' (Alison's unexpected word) had made it clear she was doing it as a favour and because you were an 'interesting proposition'. The waiting list for 'Ambleside' was long; parents of the best professional and grazier families put their girls down years ahead.

'So I hope you'll do your stuff and impress the old cow,' says Ally without great expectations in her voice.

She has parked the vehicle out of sight of the school buildings. She has got herself up for the occasion in more than the usual lipstick, her *bois de rose*, and a pair of black glacé shoes which make her limp.

As she limps ahead she mutters panting, 'Punctuality gives me the gripes, but on some occasions it pays off . . .'

The hem of the *bois de rose* is hanging. It would be unkind to tell her. Your relationship is very close this morning.

It is hard to decide which is the more melancholy, a humming school or a deserted one. A superior maid tries to make us feel inferior and does, because we are disturbing the holidays. 'Miss Hammersley has gone swimming,' she says, 'but will be back soon.'

She shows us into the head's study and leaves us to its silence, our breathing, and our fears.

It is a mellow room, paintings, books—more than you have seen since coming to Australia. Photographs of men in uniform, British to the last hair of their moustaches. Less mellow the school groups—of 'Ambleside' girls squeezed up together, with assorted teachers, and a nurse in a cap.

'That's matron,' says Ally. 'She's been here for years, doling out the castor oil. You'll miss that because you're only day.'

There's a group of girl cricketers. In the centre an elderly lady in trousers, exhibiting a bit.

'That's old Jinney in her favourite rôle.' My aunt can't resist a giggle. 'I'll laugh outright, darl, if you become a cricket star.'

Just then the maid returns, to investigate the noise, and find out whether you are lifting some of the ornaments.

She adjusts the blinds '. . . summer fades fabrics . . .' she hisses, to make her appearance look less blatant. 'Miss Hammersley will be here soon,' she assures, with a sideways look at this somewhat unorthodox candidate.

Almost immediately Miss Hammersley is.

She is still slightly moist from her dip. Her hair has this damp frizz. Obviously Jinney doesn't give a damn for hair. She is in a skirt today, askew round her bottom. Her large gold-rimmed spectacles radiate the superior virtues of the pure-bred Anglo-Saxon upper class. Actually, as a Pom, Jinney Hammersley has it over the pure-bred Anglo-Saxon Australians, who probably would not have it otherwise. Even Ally, for all her contempt, wears a slight cringe—along with the cracked glacé shoes and the *bois de rose* hem which has escaped its stitches.

She is on about her niece adapting herself to life in Australia. You suspect that Ally, if you hadn't been there, would have liked to represent you as a kind of Greek tragedy. But since you are present it isn't possible. And the Hammersley is determined to make it a jollier than jolly occasion.

She apologises for her 'swimming togs', wet and sandy, which she slings round the knob of a chair.

'At least they smell of the sea,' her glowing face splits as though for a discovery. 'You, Irene,' she pronounces the name English style as Harold does, 'should appreciate that. *Thalassa, Thalassa* . . .' cupping her chin and rather a dreamy smile, as she leans on this imposing desk.

You can't help laughing. It sprays around you. And Alison's horror reaching out towards her Greek tragedy of a niece, to protest, to protect us. If only Gil. Gil could have handled such a situation.

But the Hammersley has a forgiving smile. She does not appear to notice, or perhaps decides to interpret mirth as hysteria. She starts bringing out the snaps—Delphi, Olympia, Dodona, the Parthenon . . . 'my tour of the ancient sites . . .' and speaks some more of her hoi polloi English Greek. As she leans over you, the waves of *Thalassa* battle against a dew of armpits.

‘I don’t expect they introduced you to cricket’ she walks springily around as though making for the crease, ‘in our beloved Hellas,’ she says, ‘unless of course you have connections with Corfu. The British have left their stamp on Corfu.’

Seated again at her splendid desk, she promises ‘We’ll try you out. Cricket plays an important part—because, you see, at Ambleside we aim to function as a Team.’ She lowers her chin, making it three, ‘I don’t encourage specific girls, however gifted, to hog the show.’

Brief pause.

‘Scholastically,’ she booms, switching on her great round spectacles so that they flood the aunt with an electric glow and cause acute anxiety, ‘the curriculum aims at turning out girls with a broad humanistic view of life, through history, literature, the visual arts as well as encouraging the domestic virtues through a grounding in needlework and baking. Comprehensive in fact.’

Again Miss Hammersley pauses to contemplate her effects.

While the unfortunate Mrs Lockhart produces from a crumpled envelope a report on the candidate Irene Sklavos by her recent head Mr Warren Harbord.

Miss Hammersley’s outstretched arm, the scales of sea salt still trembling on its down, receives the document with appropriate benevolence. The spectacles are directed at it. The hand taps, the throat is cleared before tautening, the mouth is pursed, and the cheeks rather than the lips smile.

'Irene is an individualist, it seems—according to Mr. Warren? Harbord. Well, we shall see. I expect she will correct our Greek.'

Mrs Lockhart quails. 'Ireen is a very biddable girl' she offers her superior out of another country.

But the principal has no time for the guardian aunt. Again elbowing the desk her spectacles are focused on what could at last be the ideal pupil inside the unpromising material.

Never were you subjected, all at the same instant, to battery by cricket balls, blinding by the flicker of leafed dictionaries, soothed by the scent of slightly scorched Australian sponge helped from hot baking tins. You can only lower your eyes against Miss Hammersley's dreamy inspection, and hope for the best.

We are shown out by the snooty maid, while the principal remains behind, arranging paper-knives and blotters on her desk. Eating into a little finger is a ring with a dark green stone blotched as though with blood.

• • •

Several days later, Ally says with a mixture of relief and contempt, 'Waddaya know. The old girl's accepted you, Ireen. You must have something.'

Harold didn't say anything.

Date ?

Don't know why I have started keeping this rotten old diary again. Always too dangerous on any count. Perhaps 'Ambleside' has given me courage—or wearing the key on a chain round my neck. Anyone interested enough could probably fiddle at the lock with a hairpin. But the older boys are so obsessed with turning themselves into super males their imagination is leaving them. Apart from eyeing me once or twice, Harold seems to have lost interest.

Once Miss Hammersley wondered aloud what I wore on the chain. I did not enlighten her and she did not pursue the subject. The great slogan of the parents and anyone who knows about the school, is: *The girls all adore Miss Hammersley*, when she is hated by many of those outside the cricketing set.

I find her excessively—aggressively kind. The other evening when I was kept back by Miss Charteris over an essay she found 'original, but verging on the impertinent' Miss Hammersley called me as I was going down the steps. She put an arm around me as we walked down the gravel towards the gate. The day had been oppressive. The evening smelled of Pittosporum. Our figures cast heavy shadows in a brassy light.

'Are you happy, my dear,' she asked as though hoping the answer might be no.

'Oh yes, happy enough . . .' I must have sounded a breathy idiot.

'I wish you the greatest happiness' she sighed, stroking the nape of my neck.

Then she turned. I went on towards the road. I did not look back, but my antennae told me Miss Hammersley did.

What happiness is, I can't find out. Silences? Being left alone? That can become loneliness. Nearest with Gil in the arms of the great tree, in the garden which hangs above the water in Cameron Street.

Ally was right when she said people would take me up when I went to this school and she would lose contact with me. I have no intention of casting off Ally, but it's easy to drift with the current. Everything is put down to the war. War is boredom to those who are not being killed in it. Anyway, says Ally, if you're taken up by nice people—how she spits it out—you're not taking up with the GIs.

No, I'm not. Though you can't help brushing against them. Those sandy, freckled shallow-eyed boys from the Middle West. The cheeky muscular negroes. And pale molluscs of whisky-soaked officers, bulging out of their shirts and pants. You can't say the nice people up the line, parents of 'Ambleside' girls who invite you to their homes, don't see the Yanks as universal providers. You can come across a bulging officer or two delivering their cigarettes and tissues. Or some shy boy from the ranks they've got through an approved club and do their duty by giving him tea. But a girl, a shy schoolgirl, is less trouble, while satisfying their sense of duty.

From being a black reffo Greek, I am told I have something exotic about me, an olive complexion, classic features. The mirror won't let me accept these honours. I am never more than a dark blur with spots breaking out during my most difficult periods.

Trish says her parents are mad about me. It doesn't worry Trish because she isn't mad about her parents, she sees them as an accident. She can make a dimple come in a blonde cheek, the right one, and usually does it when she laughs. When I began at 'Ambleside' Trish Fermor-Jones became my friend, the counterpart of Viva Jenkins at the old public. Different however.

Poor Viva, whatever happened to her? We were going to keep up, but drifted apart, the way things happen—'nowadays,' Mrs Fermor-Jones would say.

Trish told me, you know Mummy would like to adopt you. I wouldn't give a hoot, well I mean I wouldn't mind having you around as a sister, you're so odd—different I mean. What about your father? She said it would be quite alright by him if it is what Phoebe wants. Daddy is only interested in money and success, he would only want you to do him credit, by being a stunning dresser and listening to his boring business friends, in Maxwell's world a good listener is everything.

I said I am good at listening, or rather, I can close up in my own thoughts. Trish laughed and made the dimple come. She said that isn't the same thing, they would find out, think it queer that you have thoughts of your own, and have held it against you. I asked Trish what she is interested in. Money and success. Then you are your father's daughter. Ah, she said I'd do different things with my money, I'd be a different kind of success. I asked her what, but she couldn't say, or didn't want to tell. Perhaps she didn't know. She looked rather angry.

I'd have thought Phoebe Fermor-Jones was interested enough in money and success. Trish said yes but Mummy has her principles, and committees and things, and comforts for the troops—and culture of course she's a culture fiend, that's where you come in.

Just when I thought I was becoming uncultured enough to please my cousins and almost everyone I come across.

Trish was looking at me very hard. I didn't realise she was preparing to let off a bomb. She has this lovely sleek corn-coloured hair and clear skin which the sun only faintly touches, and grey rather than blue eyes. The eyes seem to make her more trustworthy in the midst of so much blazing British blue. Perhaps I am influenced by *grey-eyed Athena*. Or Gil—were Gil's eyes grey or blue?

I am trying to remember when Trish throws her bomb. *What are you interested in Ireen?* An ordinary enough question if it wasn't so difficult to answer. I feel my black skin turning dark red as she continues looking at me and expecting a definite answer.

She caught me out well and truly. I didn't know what to answer but did. I was so nervous I let off a bomb equal to hers. 'Well' I said '*love* I think is what I'm most interested in.' Trish shrieked 'That's not very ambitious Ireen you can have it any night of the week.' 'That's different' I said 'surely that's sex isn't it?' I could have killed myself.

For a moment Trish looked as though she could really kill *me*. Her face never looked more like a sweet apple, but one I realised that had bones in it you'd find if you tried biting into the flesh. And teeth. Trish has perfect, even teeth, with transparent tips except that one, on the same side as the flashing dimple, an eye-tooth has been jostled out of place. I saw it as a fang. Phoebe is always saying we must do something about that tooth but all the good dentists are away at the war, we'll have to wait. A solution which suited everybody. Except me, as I saw this fang taunting me.

'How old fashioned you are, Ireen. Have you ever been *in love*?' I didn't know what to say, but mumbled yes and hoped she would leave it at that. Instead she kept mauling the idea—don't know what you mean, I love boys what they do to you of course I never let them go too far, and people marry, but your kind of love is only what you see at the movies and old frumpy relatives go on about boring everyone at Sunday supper.

It was Sunday and we were strolling at the bottom of the Fermor-Jones's garden in our best clothes, Trish when out of uniform already the stunning dresser, and me in a present from Phoebe, that aunt of yours hasn't a clue. All the Fermor-Jones shrubs are responding to autumn. Although it is wartime, their garden is perfectly kept, because they pay some elderly bloke to keep it in order, they always get what they want because they pay better than anyone. If the conditions had been different, not all those perfectly groomed shrubs and trees, there might have been a *transcendence* of light and air. Transcendence is something I am never sure about in Australia. It is a word I keep looking up in the dictionary while knowing about it from experience almost in my cradle, anyway from stubbing my toes on Greek stones, from my face whipped by pine branches, from the smell of drying wax candles in old mouldy hill-side chapels. Cleonaki's saints—their wooden faces worm-eaten with what I see looking back as acne of a spiritual kind. Mountain snow stained with Greek blood. And the *pneuma* floating above, like a blue cloud in a blue sky.

Trish and I have linked arms. 'Go on, tell!' She hits me in the ribs. I could be some gipsy fortune teller who has come down from the mountains with her tribe and a herd of brown goats.

Just then, Phoebe started calling from the house, 'Where have you girls got to? There are young men here waiting to be entertained.'

We went up to the chicken à la king and fruit salad with ice cream for the shy GI's on leave who had been hand-picked for her by the club. Trish kept looking at me as though wanting to share a secret we didn't have. I must have looked as blank as any of the hand-picked GI's. Phoebe noticed it at last. 'Go on Ireen,' she sounded rather angry. 'You've got a card trick or something up your sleeve.'

I heard her discussing me one evening with Maxwell, who was grumbling back through his cigar. 'She's no responsibility of mine. She's Trish's friend and your performing monkey. It's too bad if you didn't pick a winner.' He was sloshing the ice around at the bottom of his gin sling and I couldn't hear too distinctly after that. I only knew Maxwell had dismissed me from a life which revolved round a protected job which he shares with similar men. He had handed me over to women who wear attractive clothes, take lessons in French and Italian, and read library books . . .

Your families—your would-be adoptive one at Wahroonga, and your real Lockhart one at ramshackle old Neutral Bay. If anything is real in these years when we are shooting in all directions—or wrinkling and drying up. Phoebe asks, while putting on the moisturiser, 'What is that aunt of yours doing down there?' Ally at the ironing board only refers to 'Those people . . .' voice tilted upwards, expecting information. At least the Fermor-Joneses haven't access to the diary. If the Lockharts haven't either, they know about it, their eyes bore through locked drawers, it is a family joke.

Shan't write any more diary. My memory is more vivid and safer. Trish *says* she doesn't remember much of what happened before the age of eight. I can't believe it. Sometimes I think I remember Mamma throwing me out of her womb. Much of what sticks in my mind is trivial, some of it beautiful—that kingfisher clinging to the giant sunflower, weighing it down, that will stay with me for ever like some enamelled plaque. But nastiness clings to the mind more easily than beauty—those corpses of little grey mice a cat spewed on the veranda board. Bruce's hairy arm brushing mine. At least I can honestly say Bruce's arm reminds me of Gil's. Then my shudder needn't be one of disgust. Or is that dishonest? Do I wait for it to happen again? All these trivial memories are in a way more real than for instance the night the Jap submarine came inside the Harbour. Like a not too bad dream. The greatest part of it old Mrs Hetherington down the street woken by the noise falling off her bed and breaking her hip.

Phoebe sometimes puts on her religious voice to talk about historic occasions like '. . . the Jap submarines inside the Harbour, and the Battle of the

Coral Sea. I hope you girls will remember what you've lived through!' After the Battle of the Coral Sea she gives us corals to make sure. Mine is a necklet of little dark red jagged teeth, but Trish got a string of smooth beads almost white. I heard Trish complaining to her mother that they hardly looked like coral at all and Phoebe said, 'You shouldn't complain white corals are more distinguished—more valuable.' Then she added, 'I don't advise you to tell Irene. She's perfectly happy with that little necklet.' Trish has never exactly told though she did once let out that dark corals are considered somewhat common—something for tourists. Perhaps that is what I am. I don't feel I shall ever belong anywhere.

No more diary, even when my fingers itch. Thinking is bad enough without perving on what you've written down.

You are feeling virtuous this afternoon. Miss Babington has given you an Alpha for the History essay. The only other Alpha is Jinny Forster. In the beginning she wanted to be your friend. But Trish appealed, with her blonde hair and clear skin. Jinny is thin and dark, bites her nails, has spots. Angela Fallon said you were both so clever, did you use the same crib? Jinny thinks we are twin minds. You shouldn't shudder but do. At least you don't bite your nails. Trish is up against it today. She hasn't produced a history essay. Old Babs is cutting up rough, asks what her excuse is *this* time. Her parents insisted she go to visit friends across the Bridge. Babs's moustache has never looked spikier. Telling Trish she isn't interested in the social life of spoilt young women. She is here to educate them. Patricia will report to the head when school is out. Patricia looks more beautiful than ever, but the bones are visible inside the apple. She sits beside you slightly smiling, lids lowered. She has the confidence in her own worth you will always lack. On your other side, Jinny is muttering and fuming biting farther into her nails from hate and disapproval. You are caught between two opposite climates.

When school is out you hang around in front on the tessellated veranda waiting for Trish to be finished with Miss Hammersley. Jinny hangs around too, bashing her leg with her battered old case. Jinny says why don't we catch the same train. Like Lockharts the Forsters live down the wrong end of the line. You try to sound pardonable explaining that Mrs Fermor-Jones is expecting you to spend the night with them. Jinny is muttering something about everybody crawling to the rich. Then without warning, 'Are you in love with Trish, Ireen?' You can feel the spots multiplying under your burning skin. You say you don't know what she means. If she had gone off there and then, she might have started you biting your nails. Oh God, life isn't easy. You hate Trish as much as Jinny.

Trish appears at the same moment as the sun bursts through the sycamores to touch her up. Her hair has never looked a heavier gold above her forehead. Her lips are smiling contemptuously—for us? for Miss Hammersley? for what?

'What did she say?'

'She said that in a serious world the triviality of my mind ought to be punishment enough.'

Jinny spits. 'Perhaps Hammersley's palm can be greased like any other!'

She stamps off, bashing the shrubs with her old case all the way to the gate.

Trish laughs, and you see her fury. 'Bitches will be bitches. She smells too. Come on, let's go.'

'What about homework?'

'You can do that with us if you're feeling so bloody virtuous.'

Walking back to their place she tells what happened the evening before.

'They're not exactly friends of the parents, more sort of acquaintances. Phoebe warned me they're awful bores and I'd be silly to go. They wouldn't dream of driving all that way for a pot of tea and a few dry biscuits—and *she's* practically mental. But I had this idea. And after all, Fiona's my friend.'

'Fiona?'

'Yes, Fiona Cutlack. She's the niece.'

Trish's voice is growing dreamier.

'There was this dreamy boy. I'd heard enough to whet my appetite. So I put on the white corals and borrowed the Rolls—not the sacred one, but the one for the beach, that the rust's got into. Gil Horsfall was better than I could have imagined—English—his father a high ranking staff officer in India—Gil evacuated out from Home when war began. He has grey eyes.'

No blue, nothing so honest as grey.

'Actually I think they're what you call hazel. And a body. I don't know why Fiona hasn't got him under lock and key. When it was time to leave he asked if he couldn't drive the Rolls round a block or two. We started off, careering round the whole of Vaucluse, Fiona wouldn't come, said she wasn't well. I never ever was so thankful for the bloods. To have him to myself . . .'

On and on the voice till we reach Thrussell Street where you plunge down towards 'Mornington'. You remain rooted to this spot in the asphalt as everything else moves around you, Trish's voice, the over-fertilised Wahroonga shrubs, Gil taking the Vaucluse corners at a giddy speed.

If you are stunned by the brassy light of this golden afternoon, Trish is hypnotised by her own voice and the rushing of the midnight air '. . . pretty well delicious, but afraid he might crash Maxie's car . . . persuaded him to pull up beside the Gap. What if we'd driven over. There could never have been a more perfect suicide—thoughtless and perfect—better than waiting to find out somebody's bad and boring points. Instead we sat inside the car—and that was perfect too—a gale blowing outside—when Gil . . .'

You must have begun to shiver.

'What's wrong, Ireen? Are you sick or something?'

Could be. The sweat is running down your skin.

'Nothing. Could have the flu coming on. Better go home. Tell your mother I . . .'

'But come down to us. I'll ring Dr Keep.'

'No. I'm going home.'

'We'll run you there.'

'Walk a bit. Sweat it out.'

Trish obviously thinks you're quite crazy, or could she know? Not possible Gil didn't mention Eirene Sklavos, this black Greek and oddball character. As you fade away alongside this long ribbon of undulating bitumen, out of reach of Trish's eyes, if not her laughter, you will not trust anybody again.

At Turramurra where this little pocket of leftover bush fringes the road a middle-aged man unbuttons himself with his left hand. He has an iron hook where the right should be.

You hurry past. In the dwindling glare a car pulls up. An elderly clergyman offers you a lift. Says he noticed the 'Ambleside' uniform. So much respect for your Miss Hammersley, a really exceptional lady. You accept his lift, from despair as much as anything. In spite of the respect Miss Hammersley has roused in him, why should an elderly clergyman be any more reliable than a middle-aged bloke with a hook for a hand unbuttoning himself and beckoning from a pocket of bush? Anything can happen. But nothing does. He puts you down at Lockharts' gate.

'Your mother is a lucky woman.'

Oh God, can't recite family history. Thank the old boy for his kindness. You are mincing your words, simpering through these silly little baby teeth.

Nobody at home. Only the silence inside it keeps this house from falling apart, it is so fragile. The familiar objects, even in your own more or less private room, so unnecessary. Keep your hands off that diary.

Better to explode in a shower of pus than to wallow in what I expect the secure, the 'adults', would see as a stream of self pity.

An extra spurt of week-end energy gardening for neighbours, running old ladies' messages, shopping for the sick, has got Bruce his motorbike. Alison and Harold helped towards the end.

The tarnished monster stands propped on the broken concrete to the right of Alison's garage.

'It's a second-hand BSA. Can't be choosy in wartime, Reenie.'

Hardly remember what wasn't wartime, but we all act and talk as though we did. A cloud of happiness envelops what we think of as before the war.

Bruce has been working on his bike. Chrome is beginning to gleam again through the veils of baked oil and patches of rust. The rigid grid above the rear wheel is what he refers to as a pillion.

'When I've had a few practices around the place, I'll take you for a ride, Reen.'

Ought to feel grateful for Bruce's promise. He is inviting you to a celebration of power and fame. Sitting at the rear of Bruce Lockhart's bike you will act as the equivalent of the flowing figure on the bonnet of Maxwell Fermor-Jones's Rolls. What if Trish, swirled by Gil Horsfall in the Rolls, ever caught sight of you bumping along dislocated on Bruce Lockhart's pillion. But Vaucluse and Cremorne are worlds apart.

The invite is issued on one of those evenings of early winter when a razor is running its edge over the skins exposed to it, and every bay round this almost landlocked harbour is roughed into leaden waves. Regardless of a difference in hemisphere and climate, you see the same razor skinning the prisoners of war across the straits up north, when not lending a hand in cutting throats. In Greece Greeks will be dying of this wind, gunfire, and the starvation which comes from a diet of weeds.

Greeks are fated to die, when here a pseudo-Greek is only numb from the south-easter and the very remote prospect of death. Unless a crash is thrown in your way, as you cling to Cousin Bruce's ribs from the pillion of the second-hand BSA. We are on the ride to celebrate speed and status. B. has opened his mouth and is screaming into the face of the wind. You can feel his lungs expanded inside the cage of ribs. You can visualise Bruce's skeleton, from the taut ribs, and the mouth and the eye sockets, which you cannot see but know.

'Okay, Reenie?' He calls back over his shoulder.

'Okay! Okay!' We are all okay since the Yanks came.

I can feel my forehead drained white below the roots of lifted hair. Eyes staring like Bruce's in their sockets. Teeth not grinning, but clenched. Because this pseudo Australian is the crypto-Greek expecting the death which is aiming at her. But Brucie doesn't envisage death for a moment. Australians are only born to live. To end in a cemetery or crematorium doesn't bear thinking about. So you don't think. When here is this morbid Greek thinking about the death which will release her. Whamm! You are floating back rejoining the bloodstains on the Pindus snow the brains mashed into the paving outside the National Gardens the choirs of worm-eaten saints all that you have ever known and felt and cried about and prayed for, on your knees, and in cold beds.

Let Gil Horsfall stay alive in Australia, it is what he deserves.

You cling even closer to Brucie's ribs when there is no need, he is slowing down, coasting in the approach to some sort of destination.

We have arrived at this suburban mixed business with jerry-built milk bar added on. Bikes similar to Brucie's are propped in the dust and devil's pitchforks outside. The browned out light in the interior has turned the milk bar or soda fountain into a devil's cave. Brucie's mates are gathered at the bar gulping the stuff out of the metal floats, spooning up the ice cream, those of them who have scrounged or snitched cigs dragging on their loot, jerking out unintelligible information in their new, men's voices. You would like to hear and understand, but you aren't invited to come inside. No girl has been added to the circle of relaxed males stretching their thighs and their adam's apples. Only the proprietor's wife, more a priestess than a woman, sets the drinks whizzing, or drizzles from on high green or crimson synthetic flavours.

You walk about the other side of the road. It is no longer cold, but you warm your hands one in the other. They have absorbed the journey's dust and some of the grease from the BSA. Down through the lantana scrub, the jungle of gums, pittosporum and looped vines, the harbour sets up a mauve glitter.

What are you here for? Will nobody tell you what to do? You are almost mewing like one of the unwanted cats their owners dump in the suburban bush, when Bruce comes out from his magic cave, carrying one of the battered floats.

He crosses the road. 'Strawberry,' he says, and turns back.

Strawberry must be for girls, whether they like it or not. Sipping the sickly stuff is at least an occupation, even though you feel you may fetch it up. Pour the contents into the dust, but what to do with the empty float in the next half hour, or eternity.

When eternity is Gil's, Bruce and his mob have no part in it. Boring pseudo-men. And this float, with its pseudo-strawberry stickiness.

A greater raucousness in the brown mists of the cave across the road. A couple of indistinct figures are detaching themselves from the frieze strung out against the counter. Arrogance and self-importance give the giants a drunken look. They lurch out pulling up their belts, feeling their crotches.

'Hi, whataboutit?' one of them calls. All masculine confidence. The two stand there swaying and braying, thumbs hooked into the corners of pockets tighten the stuff round hips and crotches.

The second gallant has widely spaced pointed teeth, rather large, anaemic gums, and a fine fuzz on his bony chin. 'Don't tell me you're so uptight, a bloke wouldn't stand a chance of getting it in.'

They chortle for their own wit. Stumble against each other for support as they prepare to cross the road. What is both possible and impossible hangs like a pale globe above the three of us. The scrub the dusk are toppling over in a rush towards sea and the light that still skirts the bay. Bones and sticks are for breaking. Didn't the Souliot women throw themselves off the precipice?

Till Bruce elbows his way between his mate, 'Comoffut—waddaya thinken—she's me sister.'

'Go on! didn't know you had a sister.'

'. . . the relative—me *cousin* . . .'

'On with your cousin, eh?'

Their sniggers are feathered with relief. 'Cousins's allowed, aren't they?'

'Well, good luck, Brucie.'

Bruce has become a gangling amateur of a man. He has let the side down. He kicks the stand from under the bike.

'Come on,' he orders sulkily.

Doesn't sound as though he will ever forgive you for his offence against mateship.

You settle yourself as he kicks free of the stationary earth. After the first explosions, the wheels splatter some obstruction flat—the battered old aluminium float? We are toiling uphill in a cloud of fumes. Bruce's ribs have contracted inside the cold shirt. The face you cannot see has not become the skull of the outward journey human eyes will be glooming in the sockets, eyebrows ground into each other.

You would like to say something consoling to Bruce. 'Do you think she'll make the hill?' Which makes it worse.

Ally asks, 'Where have you two been?' If she condemns, there is a flicker of unwilling pride inside her condemnation—and gravy stains on what was once a pretty, floral apron. 'Your tea's in the oven—drying up fast.' She has no time to waste on kids.

Harold comes in this other evening. He is carrying an evening paper. He is out of breath from that uphill short cut he takes from the ferry, or something could have excited or frightened him out of his normal composure. He is almost at the point of telling what makes his lips tremble, but it is against his nature to give anything away if he can help it. Perhaps he has been caught out soliciting girls or he's been promoted at the Department.

He says in this funny voice, 'The Germans have had it. The war in Europe is over.'

'What—only in *Europe*?' Bruce shouts. As though Europe hadn't even been their affair. 'The war won't be over till we've socked the Japs.'

You are less than ever one of them though Alison the aunt lets out a little whimper. 'Poor Gerry!'

'Gerry?'

'My sister—your aunt . . .'

Bruce sticks out his lower lip. Above it the eyes look blank. Heard of her of course, but forgotten. No more than a name and the face in a snap. What can a dead aunt mean to the living?

Harold who is not a soak, or at any rate not in the family circle, where he makes a parade of his ginger ale, says with careful solemnity, 'This is an occasion where I propose to wet my whistle.'

Ally whose eyes have been straying towards the cupboard where she keeps her gin behind the Fowler preserving jars, throws back her head and screams through veined stringy throat. 'Never heard you use such an old-fashioned expression!'

'It's what my father used to say.'

'Your father! When you're so keen on sounding up to date.'

Harold isn't going to be deterred. He fetches out the stashed bottle of Scotch and wets his whistle. Harold who has always been bored by fatherhood except as a means of keeping Alison quiet, borrows his father's virtue, old Dr Lockhart, to help celebrate the end of the war in Europe.

Ally cries, 'Oh God!' in what is between joy and despair, and makes no secret of the gin behind the preserving jars.

When the middle boys come in they say oughtn't we go somewhere to celebrate the end of the war in Europe.

They've forgotten about you. It's your fault of course—if you don't tag on. It's the best way to be forgotten. Outside this lopsided moon is hung above the empty clothesline and the fretted vegetable leaves. Anonymous cats are taking over. The boys' laughter is swallowed up in the run towards the ferry. The little kids are breaking their toys and grizzling for their supper. A cold dew is settling on your hair.

'Ireen?' Ally calls from habit through the screen, but soon gives up to cut slices of stale sponge for her Col and Wal, and resume her whistle wetting session with her unusually considerate Harold.

Now that the war is over—the *real* war—*your* war—Cleonaki will surely write, and you will return to what belongs to you. And Gil to London? To the bomb craters and his mother's coffin, and his friend Nigel Brown's ghost. Gil himself a ghost haunting the garden on the precipice in Cameron Street, as you are haunting this mouldy back yard. Twin ghosts in the one haunting.

Is this where we belong then?

When you go in the two little boys are growing drowsy in the last stages of a squabble over the open pages of the atlas.

Gin-drowsy Ally murmurs, 'This is the kind of night when children are got. Thank God I'm past it!'

Harold of the wet-whistle and careful enunciation, 'No-one was ever cruder than Alison Pascoe when she sets out to be!' His laughter implies neither approval nor censure, as he passes plump fingers and meticulously clipped nails through the silvery hair-do.

They look only vaguely at you—at the ghost who has been haunting them.

Afterword
A Note on *The Hanging Garden*

DAVID MARR

Patrick White took one last look at *Flaws in the Glass* on the Australia Day holiday in January 1981 and posted the 'self portrait' to his publishers in London the next day. Hours later he began work on *The Hanging Garden*. As he had so often before, White would cope with the agony of waiting for his publisher's verdict by plunging into the next book.

'I have another novel coming along hot and strong in my head,' he told the critic James Stern after Christmas. Friends who heard the news in those weeks worried White was working to the point of exhaustion. He had been so ill in December he feared he would die, and there had then been terrible storms in the house on Centennial Park when his partner, Manoly

Lascaris, read the scathing portrait of his family in *Flaws in the Glass*. But White told the stage designer Desmond Digby he had no time to holiday. 'He's got to get this other novel off his chest straightaway.'

White wrote steadily through February. By happy accident, *Flaws in the Glass* was taking a long time to reach Jonathan Cape. On 20 February, Digby noted White was 'pleased with start of new novel'. There is no sign White was ever anything but pleased with his work on the book. When his writing was going badly, he would moan about it freely to friends and publishers. He had abandoned two novels in the 1960s after tearing them to shreds in his letters. There was none of that with *The Hanging Garden*. Trouble lay elsewhere.

He was old; his health was failing; he was seized with a missionary zeal to save the world from nuclear catastrophe and Australia from its Tory government – and he was falling once more under the spell of Jim Sharman. The young genius behind *The Rocky Horror Picture Show* and a string of hit musicals on the international stage had returned to Australia in the 1970s and revived White's plays to great acclaim. A deeply grateful White dedicated *The Twyborn Affair* to Sharman. Now Sharman was to direct the Adelaide Festival and asked White for a play. Time was short.

White resisted for weeks but by early March he was at work on both the novel and a play. He told the critic Jim Waites: 'I had an idea for one but had never written it, as I didn't feel anyone would be interested.' The play was *Signal Driver*.

In the crowded weeks that followed, White divided his time between the two projects. A telegram on 10 March delivered Cape's enthusiastic verdict on his memoirs, but many battles with his publishers followed to defend the sharp edge of his attacks on political and personal enemies. He was intransigent. In that same spirit he broke an old rule and appeared on television to condemn the political stagnation of his country. He was inundated afterwards with letters of support and pleas for help. With pride and exasperation he told Tom Maschler at Jonathan Cape: 'Every other day I am expected to wave a wand and save somebody or something.'

The contrast between White the writer and White the campaigner at this time is absolute. While he raged on television against the failings of contemporary Australia, he was evoking in his new novel a more innocent time in the life of his country seen not through the eyes of an angry, sick old man but two children of fine promise. The prose is assured, unhurried and disciplined. White is everywhere and absent, as only the greatest novelists can be. Though his fears left him flailing at times in public, at his desk in the house above the park he was proving, once again, to be a writer of perfect poise.

White liked symbolic deadlines. He put the novel aside in order to finish a first draft of the play by 25 April, Anzac Day. 'With all this, the novel I had begun is holding fire, but I shall come back to it as soon as I can; it is all in my head,' he told his translator, Jean Lambert. A second draft of the play followed but by early June he was rereading the manuscript of the novel. 'So far I have liked what I came across,' he told Graham Greene at Cape. 'It should be all right when I get it together. There is only this dreadful old age business, and one's dread of blindness and senility.' In August he told Maschler: 'The novel is coming along by fits and starts. I hope I have the strength to finish it.'

He wrote in blue ballpoint pen on quires of foolscap. These five bundles, each holding roughly 10,000 words, tell us little about his creative chemistry. All the hard work was done in his head, not on the page. He scratches out paragraphs here and there, but essentially the prose rolls out in a long, clean ribbon. Characters, scenes and dialogue emerge fully formed. Corrections were made in red ballpoint pen. White's handwriting, superb at first glance, has traps and hidden tangles for the uninitiated. He can hardly be reproached for this: these bundles of manuscript were meant for his eyes only.

The novel was to be in three parts, a structure White had used as early as *The Aunt's Story*. But lately he had dispensed with chapter breaks so that each section of his last novel, *The Twyborn Affair*, has the long arc of a novella. It would seem the same was planned for *The Hanging Garden*: the outer sheet of the top bundle is marked 'I' and the text is an unbroken 45,000 words, which he later told his cousin Peggy Garland amounted to 'about a third of a novel'. He had brought this part to a conclusion by October when the whole project finally came to grief in the uproar surrounding the publication in London and then Australia of *Flaws in the Glass*.

The book was front-page news. White's acerbic verdicts were quoted in newspapers throughout the English-speaking world. Attacks and counter-attacks were furious. As he approached his 70th birthday, White found he had published the great best-seller of his career. He also found these weeks fundamentally exhausting. He wrote in one or two letters of hoping to return to the novel once the furies were off his back, but in November he confessed to Maschler: 'The whole thing has left me very tired and I doubt I shall ever get back to a normal writing life.' As the year ended, he realised he had neither the stamina nor the will to 'grind out' another big novel. He announced almost formally that he would now devote what energies he had left to the stage and political causes. 'No more novels,' he told Lambert. 'They are too wearing, physically and I think by now I know how to machine gun more accurately in the theatre.'

He put the manuscript away. Perhaps he hoped to turn *The Hanging Garden* to good use one day as he had other discarded projects. 'The Binoculars and Helen Nell', abandoned in the late 1960s because it seemed 'an overblown mass, of too much flesh', was mined immediately for *The Night the Prowler* and years later for *The Twyborn Affair*. The fragment 'Dolly Formosa and the Happy Few', put aside because it 'smells a bit of carpentry and bookmaking', would be dug out twenty years later to become the backbone of *The Memoirs of Many in One*. But there was to be no such afterlife for *The Hanging Garden*. It was found untouched in White's desk at his death in 1990.

He had directed his unpublished manuscripts be destroyed. But his old friend and literary executor, Barbara Mobbs, had her doubts: if White really wanted this evidence of his long literary life to disappear, why hadn't he burnt the papers himself? Before leaving his old house in Castle Hill in 1964 he destroyed all his manuscripts and hundreds of letters in a fire that burnt for days. Many times in the last years of his life White showed Mobbs the notebooks, letters and manuscripts crammed into his desk. 'But he never told me to get the matches.' She waited for Manoly Lascaris to die; took a little more time so that everything might be done in good order; and then, on behalf of the charities that are the beneficiaries under White's will, sold thirty-two boxes of his papers in 2006 to the National Library of Australia. It proved the greatest literary treasure trove in this country.

The possibility of publishing *The Hanging Garden* was broached with Mobbs in 2010. She was sceptical but did not veto the idea. A typescript was prepared under the supervision of Professor Margaret Harris and Emeritus Professor Elizabeth Webby of Sydney University, as part of their work on the White papers funded by an Australian Research Council grant. Harris and I then checked the transcription together, leaving about twenty unreadable phrases to be deciphered by Mobbs, the greatest living expert on White's handwriting. We also enlisted the writer Angelo Loukakis and my colleague at the *Sydney Morning Herald* Anna Patty to deal with White's Greek. One impossible Greek phrase defeated us. Otherwise we ended up with a clean and unambiguous text.

It is not a first draft. White had clearly been through the manuscript at least once making corrections. Nor is it a final draft. He had left notes here and there in the text about problems – nearly all trivial – that needed to be addressed. The most substantial comes in the manuscript's last pages, where White has the news of Hitler's defeat reaching Sydney (wrongly) in the evening. He had a lifetime horror of anachronism: 'Foregoing passage on end of the war in Europe in need of revision as the news came through in the morning. First must come the address of school heads, then in the evening personal reactions of parents and children to the great event.'

Where White planned to take the novel after VE Day remains entirely opaque. I have found nothing in his letters to indicate what he may have had in mind. After he put the manuscript away he rarely mentioned it again. There is, however, a clue that Eirene Sklavos and Gilbert Horsfall might end up in contemporary Sydney. On the back page of the last of the five bundles of manuscript is this calculation in shaky ballpoint pen:

14 in 1945
50 in 1981.

Mobbs had the typescript in January 2011 and read *The Hanging Garden* for the first time. The decision to publish was taken in March. 'I'm extremely nervous of posthumous publishing, which I usually don't admire. But this is up to a very high standard and even though it is only part one, it is complete in itself,' she declared. 'I have no doubt it deserves to see the light of day.'